Emma

Woman of Faith

OTHER BOOKS AND AUDIO BOOKS
BY ANITA STANSFIELD:

First Love and Forever

First Love, Second Chances

Now and Forever

By Love and Grace

A Promise of Forever

When Forever Comes

For Love Alone

The Three Gifts of Christmas

Towers of Brierley

Where the Heart Leads

When Hearts Meet

Someone to Hold

Reflections: A Collection of Personal Essays

Gables of Legacy, Vol. 1: The Guardian

Gables of Legacy, Vol. 2: A Guiding Star

Gables of Legacy, Vol. 3: The Silver Linings

Gables of Legacy, Vol. 4: An Eternal Bond

Gables of Legacy, Vol. 5: The Miracle

Gables of Legacy, Vol. 6: Full Circle

Timeless Waltz

A Time to Dance

Dancing in the Light

A Dance to Remember

Barrington Family Saga Vol. 1: In Search of Heaven

Barrington Family Saga Vol. 2: A Quiet Promise

Barrington Family Saga Vol. 3: At Heaven's Door

Barrington Family Saga Vol. 4: Promise of Zion

a novel by

ANITA
STANSFIELD

In cooperation with
The Joseph Smith, Jr., and Emma Hale Smith Historical Society

Covenant Communications, Inc.

Cover image: *Of One Heart: Emma On the Ice* © 2008 Liz Lemon Swindle. Used with permission from Foundation Arts. For print information go to www.foundationarts.com or call 1-800-366-2781

Published by Covenant Communications, Inc.
American Fork, Utah

This is a work of historical fiction. Some of the incidents, places, and dialogue are products of the author's imagination, and are not to be construed as real.

Printed in Canada
First Printing: June 2008

15 14 13 12 11 10 09 08 10 9 8 7 6 5 4 3 2 1

ISBN-13: 978-1-59811-630-4
ISBN-10: 1-59811-631-1

For Emma,
my greatest heroine.
From your example I draw strength.

CHAPTER ONE

The Admirable Mr. Smith

Nauvoo, Illinois—1876

Emma stood alone at the edge of the Mississippi, pondering its lazy flow that was so familiar to her. A balmy breeze tugged gently at her graying dark hair, enticing it to stray from the pins that kept it tucked into a braided bun at the back of her head. She wrapped her shawl more tightly around her shoulders and closed her eyes, inhaling the constancy of the river; its smell, its sound, its very existence were among the few things that bridged the life she now lived to the one she'd known with Joseph. She loved the way the river beckoned her back in time, and she eagerly answered its call, far preferring her memories over the lonely ache that had become an ingrained part of her soul. More than three decades had passed since she'd lost her precious Joseph. She had learned to live without him; she had found solace and strength from a source beyond herself that had carried her hour to hour, day to day. But nothing had ever felt right without him. It was as if she'd not been entirely whole until he'd come into her life, and when he'd left it, he'd taken a part of her with him.

There were days when Emma pushed the memories away, for many of them were difficult, if not painful. Even the moments of perfect joy she'd spent with Joseph could, at times, only enhance her heartache over his absence. But there were other days, like today, when she encouraged the memories, finding an ironic kind of comfort in reliving the seventeen years of their marriage. A lifetime had been crowded into those years; they'd shared more joy and sorrow, more elation and misery, than most people would *ever* experience in an entire lifetime. And Emma had lived two lifetimes since without him, measuring each year as another step in bringing her closer to the day when she would be with him again. Only the promise of eternity gave her any hope at all.

"Joseph," she whispered into the breeze, and lovingly fondled the worn gold beads encircling her throat—a gift from Joseph; one of the few tangible remnants she had of his love for her. Running her fingers from bead to bead, she could easily find a tender memory to match each one, an oasis of joy in the midst of all the horror that had followed them from place to place. Still, she would not trade away those struggles for a life shared with any other man. Joseph's name was revered and honored by many, and spoken in vain by others. At times, his very greatness was difficult to comprehend; at other times, it was impossible to think of him associated with anything *but* greatness. Emma, more than anyone, knew of his humanness and his imperfections. Still, the reality of his having mortal weaknesses was further evidence of his divine mission. There was something illogically miraculous in all of it, and all the more miraculous due to the utter lack of logic. Only divine intervention could take a man of such humble circumstances and ordinary upbringing and guide him to be at the very heart of such wondrous events and unfathomable accomplishments. Emma shared the respect for Joseph that she had observed in all who encountered him, as well as an undeniable witness that he was a man of God. She knew beyond any doubt and of her own accord that he truly was a prophet. And she admired and honored the prophet with all her soul. But it was the man that she loved. For being a prophet made him a better man, and being a man, with all the necessary humanness of this mortal existence, made him a better prophet.

Those who had known him surely shared her sentiment, and yet no one knew him as she did. *No one.*

Julia stood on the deck of the ambling riverboat, distracted by the slosh-slosh sound of the enormous wheel as it pressed farther up the Mississippi, closer to Nauvoo. She longed for the security of her mother's presence, and the familiarity of home. The tragedies of her life tightened her heart and left her wondering about God's purposes. Or perhaps God had nothing to do with it at all. If she could answer *that* question, she might believe there was some tiny possibility of finding peace in whatever might be left of her life. But how could she find such answers when she wasn't entirely certain if she were running to the sanctity of home, or simply running away from her damaged existence?

Nauvoo rested quietly at the bend in the river, discarded and eerily void of the vibrant spirit that had once been bursting from every street corner and storefront, every home and farm. Julia felt both comfort and fear as she stepped off the boat, determined to put her most recent heartache behind. This place was indeed home to her, but it also represented more difficult memories than she cared to number. Clutching her satchel tightly, she hurried over a path her feet knew well, preferring to push certain memories away, disheartened when they seemed determined to surface. This had been Joseph's city; *City Beautiful,* he'd called it. But the spirit of Nauvoo had died with her father, and nothing had ever been the same for Julia—or her mother. It was impossible to walk the streets of Nauvoo and not be mindful of how it had once been. And Julia had never been able to understand why God would enable His people to build a thriving community out of a swamp—with a temple in its midst—only to have them abandon it and leave the city's founder murdered for his efforts.

But she knew well enough that such questions had no answers, so she pushed them away and hurried on.

Julia's need to feel the comfort of her mother's embrace was momentarily distracted by a desire to linger for a few minutes near a lilac bush her mother had planted many years ago. It greeted her with full blossoms and a sweet aroma that softened her mood. She closed her eyes and inhaled the fragrance, willing it into her spirit along with memories of a happier time, a time when laughter and security had been fleetingly present. Thoughts of her mother urged her on, and she took with her a significant handful of the lilacs. She lifted them to her face to again inhale their fragrance as the familiar walls of home rose before her. But it was not the structure of bricks and mortar that had lured her back; it was her mother that she needed. Emma's strength had been the one true constancy in Julia's life. And if she'd ever needed strength, she needed it now.

Julia entered the sitting room and sat down across from Emma. She'd sensed her mother's especially somber mood even before their greetings had been exchanged. She wanted to inquire over the reasons, if only to distract herself from her own misery. But she wasn't certain how to open the topic, and wondered if it was best left untouched. Emma offered a wan smile, and Julia returned it. Julia loved her mother's smile, although she'd never quite gotten used to how the sadness in her eyes contradicted it. Emma hadn't smiled with her eyes since the day Joseph had gone to Carthage. And he'd never come back. Life had been hard long before then, but it was the absence of Joseph in Emma's life that had taken the smile from her eyes.

Emma leaned back in her rocker, gazing out the window toward the river. She was looking more old and frail than when Julia had last seen her, but she remembered well the woman

Emma had once been. Taller than average, her height made her stand out in a crowd among most women. Or perhaps that was due more to the way she had carried herself, and due to an intangible aura about her that radiated something subtly remarkable. That aura was still there, Julia thought. No amount of sorrow or evidence of aging could ever change that. The black taffeta dress Emma wore, lovely as it was, seemed to declare that, in spite of the years Joseph had been gone, she still grieved his loss. Was this a day of mourning? Julia wondered. The white shawl resting comfortably over Emma's shoulders softened the severity of her dress a little, but it also drew attention to the lines of living etched into her face. Still, for all her years, Emma was beautiful. And Julia admired her as deeply as she loved her. Just being in her presence soothed something of Julia's ache. But the nostalgia evident in her mother's eyes left her uneasy. She didn't want to speak of her own heartache any more than she wanted to inquire over her mother's. But she wondered if addressing both was inevitable. Perhaps. For the moment, however, she preferred small talk.

"It's a beautiful day, Mother," Julia said, trying to sound cheerful.

Emma turned her attention to her daughter, wondering what thoughts she might be trying to disguise with talk of the weather. For many years Emma had worried about Julia. She worried about her sons as well, but Julia was the oldest of Emma's children; she had seen more of the turmoil, and would remember it more clearly than some of her brothers. And it was Julia who was here with her now. Her mother's heart had keenly felt concern for how the events of Julia's life had impacted her spirit. But she knew better than to pry, and found it prudent instead to utter a brief prayer that this conversation might flow into the dark places that were perhaps starved for daylight. It had always been difficult to talk about the painful aspects of the past. But Emma knew well enough that too much pain held inside has to overflow eventually. And perhaps Emma's own tendency toward nostalgia this day could be as much for Julia's benefit as her own.

Emma felt her prayers were being answered when the conversation flowed easily into the difficulties of the past that had merged into the heartache of the present. They spoke with tenderness and concern of Julia's brothers, and how their lives had been affected by all that the family had endured. Emma was most concerned for David, but she could hardly speak of her worry for her youngest child. He was the son that Joseph had never known, born not many months after his father's tragic death. And yet the torment in his life exceeded that of his brothers. Still, her concern was deep for all of her children, and she confessed as much to Julia.

"I should have done something more . . . something different, perhaps," Emma said, caressing the beads around her throat.

"What more could you have done?" Julia asked, taking her mother's hand. Their eyes met, and Julia added with conviction, "Mother, all my life I have watched you . . . no matter what happened . . . no matter how difficult . . . you have always done the best that you could. Your faith has never wavered." Julia looked down, and her voice broke as she added, "I wish that I could have even a portion of such faith."

"Julia," Emma said, touching her daughter's chin to lift her face, "some people believe that faith is a gift, that you either have it or you don't. I believe that . . . most of the time . . . faith is a choice."

Julia pondered the state of her own life and bristled. She felt utterly faithless. Memories rushed through her mind, as if years of her life could be mentally relived in a matter of seconds. Her first husband had been tragically killed; her second had gradually become abusive to the point that Julia had been forced to leave for the sake of preserving her own safety. Her own heartache and sense of failure were difficult to face, and she quickly got to the point. "I just don't have that kind of faith, Mother. Perhaps I just don't have the kind of strength you have . . . the strength to make that choice."

Emma paused in contemplation; a certain distance in her eyes implied that the words she would speak held great meaning, that they were intertwined with events of her past that made them personally valid and undeniably true. While Julia expected, or perhaps hoped, for some new piece of wisdom, her mother simply repeated, "Faith is a choice, Julia." She added firmly, "We must trust in the Lord enough to make that choice. He will give us the strength that we need. He *is* our strength."

Emma heard the conviction in her own voice and wondered as she often had where she'd found strength during certain events in her life. But she didn't wonder long. She knew the answer, and she knew it well. God had been with her from the start. She had felt His presence in her life long before she'd understood what constituted such feelings. The spiritual confusion of her upbringing had not halted her instinctive gravitation toward a Supreme Being who had her best interests at heart. Even as a child she had known He was there. She had *known* it.

Emma pondered her daughter's tender expression, and her memories trickled back to a day she recalled clearly, a particular moment of confusion from her early youth. The physical details of her childhood home in Pennsylvania had become vague over the years, but it wasn't difficult remembering how it felt to be there. She must have been seven at the time, but even after all these years, she could plainly see her father's stern expression while he made it clear that Emma was not allowed to pray.

As his meaning wholly sank into Emma's heart, she felt sad and afraid. But it didn't stop her from praying; nothing could. And one day her father found her praying . . . but she had been praying for him, asking God to help her father believe. Something changed in her father then. After that, they always had prayers.

And in time, Emma's father became devoted in his faith, and the two of them became very close. He taught her to do things that most men wouldn't bother to teach a daughter, but because of the time they shared in such activities, they became reliant upon each other. She loved and admired him deeply, and she'd always wanted to make her father proud.

When Emma became older and more fully able to understand her father's change of heart over the matter of prayer, she knew that he was a man who always tried to be true to his convictions, and in the process, he had taught her to do the same. He wasn't a person who did something just to do it; he had to truly believe in it. In many ways, his example had given Emma the strength she had needed to survive all she had faced throughout her life, although her father likely would not have appreciated the analogy. He'd never liked or come to terms with the way she had chosen to live her life, and it had always been a source of heartache for Emma. Still, a part of her understood. Perhaps he had sensed how hard it would be, and he'd wanted to spare his daughter from a life of difficulty and suffering. But he had never understood the things she had known in her heart that she could not deny. Even with all the hardships, she still would have chosen to live at Joseph's side, as opposed to the unhappiness and lack of fulfillment that would have surely been her lot had she not chosen to share her life with him. How could she ever regret following the convictions of her heart? It was, after all, what her father had taught her to do.

Emma would never forget the first time she had looked squarely into the eyes of Joseph Smith. It was a moment she had held tightly in her heart throughout the rest of her life. At the time, she could have had no conscious realization of the wondrous, tumultuous, utterly bittersweet life they would share. And yet it was as if his spirit had called out to hers in some unearthly way that had etched the moment eternally in her mind and in her heart.

At first she attempted to subdue her intrigue with this man, unable to overlook the fact that to all appearances, he was simple and poor. But with time, it became apparent that he was anything *but* simple. In truth, he was a man of more complexity than she had ever encountered.

Long after Joseph had left Emma alone in this world, she had only to think of that first moment when their eyes had connected—that was when the bond had begun to form. What she had felt in that moment was the very germination of what drew them together and kept them inseparable. Storms of adversity and winds of every imaginable evil had assaulted them continually through their years together. But Emma knew in the deepest part of her woman's heart that those very storms, for all of their accompanying agony, had only made them cling more tightly to each other, binding their hearts together, strengthening the irrefutable bonds between them. Even when miles, or prison bars, *or death* had kept them apart, he was always in her heart, and she in his. And it all began the moment she looked into his eyes. It was a moment she would never forget.

Emma Hale was raised on the notion of hard work, and she grew into womanhood with an appreciation of her own abilities in that regard. Her family worked together to run a farm as well as a country inn where travelers and boarders stayed, which contributed much to the family income. Calling the place an inn was likely an exaggeration, though, since it was more the sharing of extra space in their large home with those in need of a place to sleep and a couple of good meals a day. Once Emma reached a marriageable age, she quickly became accustomed to receiving attention from eligible men who stayed at the inn. But not one of them had ever earned more than a second glance from her. While she certainly had a desire for marriage and children of her own, she had concluded that she would far rather remain single than attach herself to a man who was shallow and lacking in substance. It didn't take much observation of a man—as he came and went and took meals under the Hale roof—to discern whether or not any substance existed behind a handsome face or a virile stature. Of course, her parents wanted her to marry well. They had made it clear that she should be on the lookout for a man with education. Education was important to Emma and a part of who she was, to be sure. She herself had achieved the status of teaching school. Her parents had also made it clear they wanted her to find a man who came from a family with means; someone well established in an advantageous profession. Emma's criterion was different, even if she didn't openly discuss her opinions too much with her parents—or anyone else. She had learned to take note of the way a man addressed a woman, and the degree of respect he offered to women in general—even strangers. Emma only had to look into a man's eyes to be able to recognize the signs of arrogance or ignorance that she preferred to avoid.

When Emma remained single after many young ladies in the area had married, she acquired a reputation for being too fussy. Many men had shown an interest in her and had sought to court her. But Emma wasn't interested. Her father was the one most dismayed over her attitude, but she told him that he should understand better than anyone why she should avoid fishing in shallow waters. After all, it was he who had taught her how to fish, and how to catch the good ones.

It was a crisp autumn day in 1825 when a new boarder arrived. Initially, Emma paid little attention to this poorly dressed man who went out in the morning and came back in the evening, covered with the soil of a day's labor. Then she heard her mother comment, "That Mr. Smith is a very kind man. It's too bad he comes from such a meager background."

Emma didn't give it another thought until that evening when she was helping her mother serve supper. "Oh, Mr. Smith," she heard Elizabeth Hale say, "this is our daughter, Emma."

Emma heard a chair sliding and turned to see this Mr. Smith come quickly to his feet—something many men wouldn't bother to do when being introduced to the woman serving their meals. She first noticed that he *was* tall and handsome, with thick, brownish hair and eyes that were unmistakably blue. Her second thought was that he had an air of refinement about him that starkly contrasted with the way he was dressed. It was almost as if he were in disguise. The effect increased when he nodded and showed a slight smile, saying with perfect respect, "Hello, Miss Hale. A pleasure to meet you." His gaze connected with hers, and she momentarily wondered if her theory of being able to judge a man's character by his eyes was truly valid. She certainly saw no signs of arrogance or ignorance.

"Mr. Smith," Emma said in a formal reply, preferring not to give him any hint as to her intrigue with him. She knew absolutely nothing about him.

That night Emma had trouble sleeping, and she wondered why. There was no logical reason why her thoughts would be so preoccupied with a man she'd barely met. She felt both intrigued and afraid. She'd simply never encountered such feelings before. Of course, there was no reason to be concerned over what to do about it. Only time would prove whether or not getting to know this Mr. Smith better was a worthwhile endeavor. She'd always been cautious and prayerful; it wasn't in her nature to be otherwise. Still, she couldn't suppress a girlish giggle that escaped her with no warning.

"What are you laughing about?" her sister mumbled in a sleepy voice. Tryael was a couple of years younger than Emma, and she was her only sister still unmarried.

"Nothing," Emma said. "Sorry." Then she pressed the pillow over her mouth to muffle *another* giggle.

By morning, Emma had firmly scolded herself for being so silly. She was a grown woman with sound intelligence. Fits of girlish delight would have no bearing on her willingness to give any amount of time to a man who did not meet her standards of minimal criteria. Money and education were not necessarily high on that list, even though she knew her father would strongly disagree. But Emma knew how to work hard, and she had no problem doing so by the side of a man who knew how to do the same. Emma wanted a husband with integrity, and steadfastness in living by that ethic. She wanted kindness and respect, and a man who believed in God and prayed—as she did. She couldn't imagine allowing her own children to be raised by a man who did not make God a high priority in his life. Truthfully, she knew nothing about this Mr. Smith in regard to such things. Compelling blue eyes and a few words spoken in kindness were no measuring stick.

Reasoning that she needed opportunity to learn whether this man had any genuine merit, Emma maneuvered herself to be in the very spot he would be required to pass in order to be served his breakfast. Her stomach quivered when she saw him coming, even though she pretended to be distracted with a menial task.

"Good morning, Miss Hale," he said in a voice that moved her for reasons that were impossible to define. She imagined that great men like Moses and Abraham would have spoken with such a voice, then she immediately pondered the source of such a thought.

"Mr. Smith," she said, exactly as she had said it the previous day. But the way he smiled led her to believe that she wasn't portraying her intended indifference.

For days, Emma exchanged little with Mr. Smith beyond trivial greetings. But her discreet observations of him were something she took seriously to heart. She couldn't deny that she was nothing but impressed with him in every regard. On a comfortably warm day, Emma stepped on to the porch to shake out a rug at the same moment Mr. Smith was approaching the house after a long day's work. Emma's heart quickened when she realized who it was. They exchanged a smile and a long gaze as he kept walking, and Emma resisted the urge to crane her neck in order to avoid breaking eye contact. Long after he'd gone inside, she felt giddy. No, it was more than that; *deeper* than that. Asking herself *what* she felt, she was surprised by an unexpected rush of emotion that stung her eyes with tears. She quickly suppressed them, not wanting her mother to be alerted to her feelings. She wasn't ready to discuss it—at least not yet.

Emma exchanged no words with Mr. Smith that evening, but the following morning, after breakfast, she was surprised to turn around and find him there. "Hello," she said.

"Hello." He smiled, and his blue eyes twinkled. "I was wondering . . . Miss Hale, if . . ." Emma realized he was nervous, and she fought not to let out a little burst of laughter at the evidence that she had the same effect on him that he had on her. He cleared his throat and continued. "Would you do me the honor of taking a walk with me this evening, Miss Hale?"

Emma was grateful for her earlier, perceptive observations, which made it easy to say, "I would like that very much, Mr. Smith. Thank you."

"That's *Joseph* Smith," he said. "In case . . . you were wondering."

Emma didn't tell him that she *had* wondered, or that the name suited him so well. She just smiled, actually feeling so overcome that she didn't know *what* to say. She was relieved when he added, "I'll look forward to this evening, then." He smiled again and was quickly off to meet his fellow workers.

When evening came, Emma found Joseph waiting near the front door, cleaned up and looking more put together than she'd ever seen. They exchanged conventional greetings and stepped outside, where he motioned with his arm and said, "You choose which way to go. I'm certain you're more likely to know the most pleasant route for a walk."

"Very well," she said and led the way.

"You've lived here for many years," he said.

"I was born here," she told him. "And where are you from, Mr. Smith?"

"New York," he said.

"You have family there?"

"I do."

"Tell me about them," she said and slowed her pace now that they weren't so close to the house.

Joseph ambled beside her and spoke comfortably about his parents. It was evident he'd come from a good family, and that their bonds were strong. They had that in common. She asked about his siblings, and he told her their names and ages, and a little about each one, starting from the youngest.

"Are you the oldest, then?" she asked when he paused at mentioning himself.

"No," he said with more sobriety, "my older brother Hyrum and I are very close. He takes good care of me."

"Then *Hyrum* is the oldest?"

"He is now," Joseph said. "Our oldest brother, Alvin, died . . . a couple of years ago."

"I'm sorry to hear that," she said and resisted taking his hand. She instinctively wanted to offer some gesture of comfort, but knew that it would be far too forward. "Tell me about him," she pressed.

Joseph smiled faintly and began to speak of Alvin, but his mood remained somber, even while he reminisced about the good times he had shared with his brothers prior to Alvin's death. He concluded by saying, "He was very good to me. He watched over me with great care, and no matter what, he always . . ."

Emma heard him stop abruptly, as if he had been about to say something and then changed his mind. "What?" she asked, not wanting him to feel embarrassed or shy about sharing something tender with her.

He cleared his throat subtly and finished, "He always believed in me."

"That's nice," Emma said.

"Now, enough about me. Tell me about *your* family."

Due to his staying at the inn, Joseph was aware of Tryael and Reuben, who were both younger than Emma. She told him about her six older siblings—four brothers and two sisters—all of whom were married, and she expounded on the love she felt for her family and the relationships they shared. He showed genuine interest and asked many questions, then the conversation moved on to other things. They ended up at the edge of the river, where they just sat and talked comfortably of things they enjoyed doing. She talked of her love of horses and her expertise in riding due to many years of practice.

"What else do you do exceptionally well?" he asked with a good-natured laugh, "so that I can be warned against embarrassing myself?"

Preoccupied by her growing admiration for this Mr. Smith, Emma gave an answer that she considered humorous—if only to herself. "I'm quite good at fishing," she said. It *was* a true statement, even if she wasn't exactly thinking of catching fish.

"And who taught you to fish, Miss Hale?"

"My father," she answered. "We've always been close. That's probably why I have so many opinions."

"I admire that in a woman," Joseph said.

"That I know how to fish?" she asked and laughed.

"No." He chuckled as well. "That you have an opinion."

CHAPTER TWO

As they started walking back toward home, Emma noticed, not for the first time, that Joseph had a slight limp. Although barely noticeable, she couldn't help being curious. Deciding their conversation thus far had been comfortable, she hoped he wouldn't be offended when she mentioned it, but she made it clear, "You don't have to tell me the reason if you don't want to."

"I don't mind telling you," he said, "although it's rather a gruesome story." His lighthearted tone dissipated as he matter-of-factly told her of a series of incidents regarding his health that had led to the need for a difficult surgery on his leg, where a portion of bone had to be removed. "My father held me through the surgery," he mused, a sober crease in his brow. "I think that I knew everything would be all right as long as he held me."

Emma pondered his statement and the obvious trust he had in his father. She understood that feeling well. It was certainly a point of common ground.

"How old were you?" she asked, horrified to think of a child enduring such a painful procedure.

"Seven," he reported, and she let out an astonished gasp.

"It must have been so traumatic!"

"Yes, but . . . my family took very good care of me, and God gave me the strength to get through it well enough. I used crutches for about three years, but as you can see, it all turned out fine."

Emma listened carefully to his words and wondered if he knew that she was consciously assessing his character. His attitude about his childhood trauma impressed her, but she was even more impressed by his mention of relying on God. She took the opportunity to say, "So, you believe in God, Mr. Smith." She couldn't think of a question to ask that might be any more important than this. At least not to her.

She took another step before she realized that he had stopped walking, and she turned to face him. "Yes, Miss Hale," he said with a conviction that almost made his voice quiver, and his eyes glistened to the point that she nearly expected him to cry. "My knowledge of God's existence is more profound than any other knowledge that I possess."

Stunned and deeply touched, Emma didn't know what to say. She could tell him that she agreed, but even for all her firm belief, she couldn't share such stout conviction. He started to walk again, and she was glad for some moments of silence to contemplate what he'd said—and how he'd said it. She was looking forward to getting to know this man much better. She could only hope he shared her sentiment.

"I'm glad your leg healed all right," she finally said.

"So am I." He chuckled as he added, "I could race you home if you'd like proof."

Emma laughed softly. "Perhaps next time."

Joseph smiled, and she wondered if he was equally pleased over the prospect of there being a *next time.* "Just as well," he added. "I'll need to prepare myself for the likelihood that you'll probably beat me."

"It's possible," she said, and they laughed together.

The next time Emma went for a walk with Joseph, she declined his challenge to run a race, but he agreed to *her* challenge to try to beat her on horseback. He stuck to the challenge even after she'd informed him that she had more than a little experience with horses and a certain knack for horseback riding. After a few days and another long walk, they found an opportunity for their race.

Emma *did* beat him, but she reminded him in all fairness that she'd had a great deal of practice. "And," she said as he took hold of her waist to help her dismount, "I may have given you a slower horse."

"Or," he drawled, "I may have let you win."

"You keep telling yourself that, Mr. Smith, if it will make you feel better."

That evening Emma's father pulled her aside and made no effort to hold back his feelings. "I don't like your seeing that man."

"Why not?" she asked. "He's been very kind, and—"

"He's not right for my daughter," Isaac Hale asserted. "It's bad enough that he's dirt poor and has no education to speak of, but I've heard rumors . . ."

"Rumors?" Emma echoed. "I've never paid any heed to idle gossip, and neither should—"

"I've had folks telling me I shouldn't even let him stay here, Emma. There's too much strangeness in what I'm hearing." He pointed a finger at her. "There's no good to be had in showing yourself in public with a man like that."

Emma felt stunned. Disagreeing with her father was so rare that she hardly knew how to respond. Isaac was clearly angry, but Emma felt too strongly about Joseph not to make a stand. "I'm not going to let what other people are saying sway my decisions, Father. I *will* see him if I choose."

"I do *not* want you seen with a man like that," he countered. "You'd do well to end it now."

End what? Emma wanted to say. For all that anyone knew—including Joseph—there had not been enough of anything between them to warrant an *end.* She wondered if telling Joseph that she would no longer spend time with him might cause him any distress. She suspected it would. And, equally important, her decision would certainly cause *her* distress. She'd grown very fond of his company, and found him worthy of her admiration.

Emma tried not to wonder what kind of gossip her father had heard about Joseph. She couldn't imagine it being anything terribly serious. For all that she could see—and sense—he was not the type of man to be attached to any kind of scandal. Considering herself a woman of good instincts and sound discernment, she pushed the matter out of her head, determined to get to know Joseph Smith a little better before she passed any judgment.

Emma *did* continue to see Joseph, even though her father did not approve of his lack of education, nor did he fancy his daughter being seen with a man who came with strange gossip attached to him. Emma felt no qualms in either case. She could outride him on a horse any day of the week. She taught him to dance, and he often joked about how she was a refining influence on him. But she believed it was the other way around. She was in awe of him, and she was falling in love with him—even if she wasn't yet willing to admit to such feelings.

Emma was disappointed when Joseph had a change in employment and went to work for a Mr. Knight, who owned a farm and grist mill across the border in New York. But Joseph told her that Mr. Knight was a good and generous man, and he proved to be so when he frequently lent Joseph his cutter so that he could visit Emma.

In a way that was typical of the time they spent together, Emma took in the pleasantness of a sunny afternoon while she walked at Joseph's side. It was easy to ignore the cold of winter when they were together. To fill the silence, she asked, "Have you ever dreamed of doing something grand? Traveling the world . . . making a difference?"

Joseph responded thoughtfully. "I would like to believe that I can make a difference in this world."

"How?" she asked with a zeal that seemed to take him off guard. But she couldn't help wondering if their dreams might coincide.

He gave her a sideways smile. "That remains to be seen, I suppose."

His ambiguous answer made her wonder if she were being too forward. She attempted to explain herself. "Mother says that I'm like Father; too many dreams, and too many opinions."

"I admire that in a woman," Joseph said, and he clearly meant it. How could she not be pleased?

They walked in silence for a few minutes, but even with the lack of conversation, Emma didn't feel at all awkward or uncomfortable. In truth, she felt an illogical level of comfort with him that was impossible to define.

The quiet was broken when he said, "I'm growing rather fond of your company, Miss Hale. I hope it's all right to admit that."

Emma smiled. "I'm growing rather fond of yours as well, Mr. Smith."

Joseph smiled in return, but his smile quickly faded, and he looked down. "I'm well aware, however, that your father holds *no* fondness whatsoever for me."

Emma ventured to say, "He's heard some . . . rumors."

"Ah, I've heard those as well," Joseph said, but he offered no explanation.

With the subject open, Emma took the opportunity to speak freely. "Personally, I don't pay attention to gossip. And since Father isn't here right now, I'm just going to enjoy myself."

"What an excellent idea, Miss Hale," he said and took her gloved hand into his. They shared a warming smile and a lengthy gaze, and Emma wondered if he knew how much she had grown to care for him. And her admiration only deepened more each time they were together. She could only pray that with time her father would soften his opinion of Joseph. Otherwise, she couldn't imagine what she might do.

Emma was startled the first time she heard for herself the rumors about Joseph. She wasn't one to indulge in idle talk or fall for malicious prattle. But stories continued to come repeatedly to her ears until it was impossible to ignore them. She often found herself lying awake at night wondering. Or her mind would wander while she went about her daily tasks. She found it difficult, if not impossible, to reconcile the Joseph Smith she had come to know as some kind of heretic lunatic who claimed to have seen angels. And then there was talk of some kind of gold Bible that he intended to dig up and translate. It all seemed far too strange for a man who possessed such natural common sense. She had every reason to believe he was a reasonable and prudent man. It simply didn't ring true. When the matter became her most prominent thought, Emma wondered if she should just come right out and ask Joseph. If he didn't bring it up eventually, *she* certainly would. But for now, she felt more prone to allow him the opportunity to speak to her about it if he chose. He surely had to be aware of the rumors—and their source. For the time being, she preferred to simply enjoy his company in an entirely uncomplicated way.

Emma had become so accustomed to ignoring all she'd heard about Joseph that she was surprised when he finally brought it up. They'd just finished eating a picnic lunch that Emma had prepared, and the woods surrounding them provided a pleasant atmosphere. When he sat to face her with a purposeful aura, she realized he was nervous. In truth, she'd never seen him so nervous. Her heart quickened to consider what might be so critical. The most logical possibility occurred to her, and she wasn't at all surprised to hear him say, "The . . . rumors you've heard . . . I need to tell you that . . . what you've heard . . . at least some of it . . . is true."

Emma took in his words with combined awe and caution. *True?* Could it be possible? But what other possibility might there be? That he *was* a heretic lunatic? She knew *that* wasn't true. Still, she carefully considered how to respond. For all of her anticipating this conversation, she had not anticipated how to answer such a question.

Before she *could* answer, he added, "If I had not experienced what I have, I might not believe it myself."

Emma had no idea how long she sat there, gazing into his eyes, unconsciously certain that she might find every answer swimming within them. She might have chided herself for getting caught up in capricious fancy, but she had enough self-awareness to recognize—even in the midst of such compelling emotions—that what she was feeling went much deeper than that. She didn't fully understand what was happening, but she knew how she felt. And it was *not* capricious at all.

Emma took a ragged breath but couldn't speak. With all the thoughts whirling around in her head, it would have been impossible for her to explain what she was feeling and have it make any sense.

During a contemplative silence, Emma considered what he'd told her, and how difficult it must have been for him to say it. She thought of the things she'd heard. *Visions and angels?* How could it be? Yet there was no doubting his own belief that it was true. And she wanted to believe in *him.* At the very least, she could be open-minded. Looking again into his eyes, she felt compelled to say, "Tell me."

"Oh, Emma," he began, but his eagerness visibly faded behind immediate trepidation.

"What is it?"

"I fear that . . ."

"What?" Again she encouraged him.

She saw firm resolve overtake his countenance. "Perhaps I should clarify something." Emma nodded, eager for any clarification he might give her. "I hold no doubt over the matters I need to share with you, Emma. But I know that . . . once I tell you these things . . . nothing will ever be the same between us."

"Tell me," she repeated, and sensed him drawing courage.

"Some years ago . . . in my fifteenth year," he began, and his resolve deepened, "I became very troubled by the many different religious sects, and the contentious attitudes among them. I believed that many of their doctrines didn't make sense . . . or feel right." He paused and asked, "Have you ever felt that way?"

Emma didn't have to ponder the question long. She knew exactly how he felt. But she was a young lady with no power to sway or influence religious concepts. And so she'd always kept quiet about such feelings, focusing instead on her personal relationship with God as opposed to being too concerned about the doctrines and sermons being discussed around her. Considering her own feelings—feelings she'd barely allowed to be entertained by conscious thought—her admiration of Joseph deepened immediately. To have pondered these concepts at such a young age seemed truly remarkable in her eyes.

With conviction, Emma answered, "I have, yes."

"It just seemed to me," Joseph went on, visibly more relaxed in proportion to his obvious conviction, "that every preacher had dramatically differing views, and there was so much contention among the members of the different sects. To me, it didn't seem at all right for people professing to be Christians to behave in such ways."

Again Emma agreed, but she only nodded to encourage him to continue.

"The passing of time only made my concerns more intense, until the matter consumed my thoughts night and day. I read in the Bible that any man who lacks wisdom should ask of God." He chuckled gently. "I knew that if anyone lacked wisdom, it was certainly me. So I determined that I would pray for an answer. I went into the woods early one morning, and . . ."

"What?" Emma pressed anxiously when he hesitated.

"Emma," he tightened his hand over hers, his eyes openly pleading. "I ask you to hear me out . . . with an open heart."

"I will," she whispered, unable to comprehend what he might tell her, but fully enraptured by what she'd already heard.

Even with the rumors that had come to her ears, and his brief admittance that some of them might be true, she was still completely unprepared to hear him say in a voice of hushed reverence, "Emma . . . I saw God the Father, and His Son, Jesus Christ."

Emma became conscious of her heart pounding the same moment she saw a hint of tears glistening in Joseph's eyes. She sucked air into her lungs and was unable to let it go. Her eye contact with Joseph remained intense while thoughts and memories tumbled through her mind and spirit. She recalled when she'd first asked him if he believed in God. She would never forget the conviction of his answer, nor the way it had affected her. He hadn't told her that he *believed.* What had he said? He'd told her that his *knowledge* of God was more profound than any other knowledge he possessed. She understood now. Or did she? It was difficult if not impossible to *comprehend* such a miracle. But surprisingly, she didn't find it difficult to *believe.* For reasons she could never explain, believing this was true felt as natural as accepting her own existence on the earth.

While he was obviously waiting for some kind of reaction, she simply asked, "What was it like?"

"Oh, Emma!" His countenance brightened, and his eyes took on a distinct glow. "It was beyond any earthly comprehension.

There is nothing I know of in this world to compare. Their brightness and glory defy all description."

"What did they look like?" she asked, realizing her perception of God was too vague and obscure to even define.

"Heavenly beings," he said. "Men . . . standing in the air . . . Father and Son . . . with bodies as we have, but glorified; perfect."

Emma thought for a moment, taking the time not just to hear what he was telling her, but to consider what she was hearing. If this was true—and she had no reason to believe that it wasn't—then she had to contend with accepting that much of what she'd been taught all her life was *not* true. Knowing it would take time to assess all she was learning, she focused on the conversation at hand. "And did they answer your prayer, Joseph?"

"They did," he said quietly. "They spoke to me . . . by name." His voice quavered. "I was told to join none of these churches, for they were all wrong—an idea that had never occurred to me."

Emma was grateful for long moments of silence that allowed her to take in the magnitude of what he was asking her to believe. While she gazed into his eyes, searching there for added evidence that he truly believed what he was saying, she wondered if he could see in her eyes her sincere desire to understand and believe it too. In her mind, Emma quickly gathered everything she had come to know about Joseph through their association, and she added to that the way she had always felt so thoroughly comfortable with him. She had no logical reason to believe that he would make up something like this and expect *her* to believe it. Such an idea was simply not in his character. But all logic aside, she could not dispute the warmth she felt. It was not as dramatic as a thunderbolt, nor as direct as blinding sunlight, yet in its still, small way, what she felt was equally undeniable.

Emma pulled away from the examination of her own feelings to assess Joseph's expression. The firmness of what he believed was readily evident, and so was his anxiety regarding her reaction. While she was searching for some words of reassurance, he said firmly, "Take some time, and consider what I've told you, Emma. God heard and answered my prayer. He will answer you. It is possible for you to know for yourself."

Again Emma's admiration for him deepened. He was not expecting her to decide in this moment whether or not she could believe or accept such unbelievable things. And he was not asking her to simply believe in these things by his word alone. That in itself let her know that he understood the nature of God's communication with His children. Emma had always felt God guiding her life, speaking to her through her thoughts and feelings. She could never have tolerance for being expected to accept *any* matter without careful prayer. And he was right. God *would* answer her. She knew that He would. Perhaps He already had, but it was certainly prudent to give the matter some time.

As long as they were having this conversation, Emma ventured to have other questions answered. "I've also heard something about . . ." She hesitated, thinking it sounded so ridiculous.

"A gold Bible?" he asked, filling in her thought exactly.

She nodded. "Is there any truth to that?"

Joseph smiled and looked down for only a moment, then he met her gaze again. "Some time after that first vision, a heavenly messenger appeared to me in my room at night. He told me his name was Moroni." Emma trembled from the inside out at what she was hearing, as much in awe as a child seeing snow for the first time, or seeing the sun break through storm clouds in brilliant streams of light. Eagerly she took hold of each word as he spoke. "While he'd lived on the earth, Moroni had been the keeper of an ancient record . . . a book . . . written on gold plates."

"So it's true," she whispered.

"It's true that these gold plates exist. They contain the history of former inhabitants of this continent and the fullness of the everlasting gospel as the Savior delivered it to those people. Moroni taught me many principles and quoted many prophecies from the Old Testament. He returned three times and repeated everything with exactness, each time adding a little more."

"Do you have these plates, then?"

"No, but I've seen them. In time I will be allowed to take them out of the place where they are kept. For now I must wait . . . and prepare."

Emma attempted to merge the Joseph Smith she had come to know with all she had just learned about him. She wasn't surprised at how well everything came together so comfortably. Realizing the source of the rumors and gossip, she said, "This must be very hard for you . . . to contend with what people are saying."

His chuckle came again, as tense as it was good-natured. "I've sometimes wondered if I should have kept my experiences to myself. I was young and naive—perhaps I still am. But I had felt certain that the local ministers would be thrilled to hear that such a glorious event had occurred. I felt no qualms about telling my story, because I knew it was true, and it simply hadn't occurred to me that others might not believe me. My family believed me; they've stood by me without question. But others did not. And once such a story has come to the ears of the public, it will only spread and will certainly never cease. Perhaps the Lord's plan for me could not be accomplished without word spreading. I must trust in Him."

"So you must," she said, surprised to find that he was still holding her hand. "It must be difficult; people can be so cruel."

He smiled as if there was some amusement on that count, or perhaps it was more an indication that he'd come to accept that it was true. Still, she was surprised and duly impressed to hear absolutely no hint of malice or anger when he said, "Some people have been *very* cruel; there have even been attempts against my life, but—"

"People have tried to *kill* you?" She couldn't believe it!

"It would seem that way," he said with easy nonchalance. "But I'm certain that as long as God has a purpose for me to accomplish—which would appear to be readily evident—I will be preserved and protected."

"I'm certain you will," she said.

When he seemed to be done, Emma felt certain she'd not heard nearly all of what he would like to share with her. But what she *had* heard felt overwhelming and difficult to take in. Not knowing what to say, she was relieved when he reiterated softly, "Pray, Emma . . . and you will know."

Emma nodded in response, too overcome to speak. Total silence fell between them until Joseph cleared his throat and said, "Would it be presumptuous of me to hope that you'll be willing to see me again?"

She smiled and squeezed his fingers, saying easily, "I'll look forward to it."

She hadn't realized how concerned he'd been about that until he let out a relieved breath, mingled with a chuckle. "Oh, I'm very glad to hear it."

"Were you afraid that I wouldn't?"

"My dear Miss Hale," he said with a sideways smile, "I have been worried about this conversation since the day I met you."

Emma leaned toward him slightly. "Now you know all that worrying was for nothing." She chuckled and added, "Perhaps you should have more faith, Mr. Smith."

"Perhaps I should," he said and kissed her hand, watching her eyes as he did. Considering all he had confessed to her, and all that she felt, she wondered why she, of all women, would be blessed with such a privilege.

Long after Joseph had walked her to the door and bid her good evening, Emma continued to wonder. She went about her chores and routine almost in a daze, recounting in her mind everything Joseph had told her, and the way it made her feel. That night and throughout the following days she prayed fervently to know, beyond any doubt that what she believed to be true actually was. With time she *did* receive an answer that affirmed to her the truth of these things beyond any possibility of doubt. With the undeniable strength of her answer, she also realized that in her heart she had known it to be true all along. When Joseph had spoken to her of his visions, she'd had no difficulty accepting them as truth. But even long before that, when she'd first heard the rumors, she'd never once felt concerned over them. It was as if her spirit had sensed the verity of Joseph's experiences long before her mind had understood the matter. And now the two were in complete agreement. She knew with absolute sureness that what Joseph had told her was true.

"It *is* true," Emma said aloud, tossing her words into the breeze for no one to hear while she was gently swinging back and forth in the rope swing near the house. A tiny fit of delighted laughter followed the statement, an expression of the perfect joy that she felt in being privy to such wonders, and to feel as she did for the man who had experienced them. Then a thought occurred to her, and she pressed her feet to the ground, which abruptly halted her swinging. Her grip tightened around the ropes, and she had trouble drawing breath. In accepting these things to be true, she also had to accept what it meant. *Joseph Smith was a prophet of God.*

An unfathomable miracle had occurred in the very time and place where she was living her life. And it had happened to the man she loved. And yes, she *did* love him. Now she could see that she'd known *that* truth all along as well—not just in the sense of romantic notions and undeniable attraction that were certainly present, but in a sense so deep it was difficult for her to grasp. It was as if the first time she had looked into his eyes, her spirit had been drawn to his, and they had connected somehow. She could never explain. She only knew that it was true. He was a prophet, and she loved him. She didn't know how it was possible; she only knew that it was. She also knew that choosing to share her life with such a man would inevitably bring hardship.

She had a sense that Joseph's mission, whatever it might entail, was only beginning. And the persecution that Joseph had already endured was surely just beginning as well. Her father's dislike of Joseph was not likely to dissipate, especially considering the fact that the rumors that had riled Isaac Hale were actually true. But Emma knew in her heart that God meant for her to be by Joseph's side. And with that knowledge, which was every bit as sure as her knowing that Joseph's visions were real, she knew that God would be with them.

Emma looked forward to seeing Joseph, anxious to tell him what she had come to learn for herself. He came with Mr. Knight's cutter and took her for a ride through freshly fallen snow that gave the surrounding woods and meadows a magical appearance. As the little sleigh glided gracefully along, they talked of trivial things and laughed together while Joseph held the reins to guide the single horse. Then he shifted the reins into one hand and took hold of hers with the other, smiling at her as he did so. When he stopped the cutter near the river and helped her down, Emma knew this would be the perfect time and place to say what needed to be said.

"What a beautiful day," she said, looking around, oblivious to the cold.

"It is, indeed," he said, but he was looking at *her.*

Emma returned his smile and took her chance. "I've been thinking about what you said . . . and I *did* pray . . . as you asked me to."

"And . . ." he said in a quiet voice, showing the vulnerability she'd seen when he'd first confessed his visions.

"I believe you," she said, surprised at the emotion she heard in her own words.

She saw Joseph close his eyes, heard him draw in a long, sustaining breath, and she could well imagine—especially after all the ridicule and disdain he'd endured—that her answer was deeply important to him. "Everything?" he asked, looking at her again.

"Everything!" she said firmly and without hesitation.

He chuckled softly and looked down. After a moment of silence she realized he was trying to hide his emotion. She set aside any concern of propriety and touched his chin to lift his face to her view. "It's all right," she said gently.

He chuckled again, sounding mildly embarrassed. As if to explain, he said, "I'm very grateful. It means more to me than I could ever tell you."

"I don't think you need to tell me," she said, then realized the mood between them had become far too somber. Impulsively she grabbed a handful of snow and threw it at him before she ran away laughing, certain he would retaliate. She heard him laugh as he followed after her, and she called over her shoulder, "Now's your chance to prove to me how well that leg has healed."

"Oh, a challenge?" she heard him call, and he quickly caught up with her.

He didn't retaliate, but just took her hand to stop her. "Emma," he said, and she turned to face him, breathless even before he added, "Thank you . . . for being such a good friend to me."

Emma smiled. "It's the easiest thing I've ever done."

She wasn't intentionally trying to be coy, but she felt an intensity regarding their ongoing exchange that was almost as acute—in a different way—as when he'd sat her down and shared his visions. She felt overcome with her own emotions, and perhaps close to tears herself. She eased away from his reach, and he followed her into the woods.

"I came here often as a child," she said.

"I'm certain you were a beautiful child," he said, and took both her hands into his. Her focus shifted to him as he added, "You're a beautiful woman."

"You don't strike me as the flattering type," Emma said lightly, if only to soften the intensity of his compliment.

"I'm not," he replied, entirely sober. His voice softened. "I love you, Emma."

Hearing his words, Emma took a sharp breath, and before she could think of how to tell him she felt the same way, she realized he intended to kiss her. She eagerly accepted his kiss with a sense that it somehow bound them together. In her heart, she knew that God had brought them into each other's lives, and that from this moment forward, nothing would ever be the same for either of them.

"I love you too, Joseph," she said. He smiled and kissed her again. It was meek and unassuming, filled with tenderness, and utterly sweet.

They walked hand-in-hand back to the cutter, where Emma enjoyed sitting close to him beneath the blanket spread over their laps while he drove the horse at an exhilarating speed. But then, just *being* with him felt exhilarating.

Back at Emma's home, they warmed up by the fire, and she thought of how she could spend her entire life in the presence of this man, feeling this way. They completed their time together with a lengthy conversation as he shared with her more depth and details of his experiences leading up to and following his remarkable vision. He spoke of the strong spiritual climate in the home where he'd been raised. Reading from the Bible and discussing its principles had been commonplace. But his parents had not been in agreement over the matter of organized religion. Joseph's mother had strong feelings about being connected to a religious body, while his father had preferred to remain aloof, believing there was something missing. Joseph told Emma that his search for the truth had surely been fueled by the concerns of his parents, but looking back, he believed that God had prepared *them* to be a part of the work that was unfolding. Emma talked with Joseph about the issues of faith and prayer in her own home, and again—not surprisingly—they found common ground, and the bonds between them deepened as their understanding of each other became more and more evident.

After Joseph reluctantly ended their visit, needing to travel many miles to return to Mr. Knight's home, Emma was once more faced with her father's disdain for Joseph. "You're spending far too much time with him, Emma. I've heard too many things about that man to ever believe there's any good to him. He's a fool and a dreamer, declaring visitations from angels and—"

"But what if the things we've heard about him are true, Father?" Emma asked, certain she could appeal to him with the same conviction she had felt when Joseph had told her. "Wouldn't it be a glorious thing if such revelation were—"

"True?" he echoed with a bellowing astonishment that filled the house. "If you're fool enough to even *consider* believing such madness, then you're as big a fool as he is."

Emma had trouble believing that *her* father—her friend and confidant all these years—would say such a mean thing to her. With tears she couldn't hold back, Emma tried again. "Father, if you would just . . . listen to me. Let me share with you the things that—"

"I don't want to know anything about it, Emma; not another word!" He shook his finger. "Be careful where you step, child. You might not like where you end up."

He left the room to close the argument. Emma sat down and cried. She felt utterly torn. She knew the path God wanted her to follow; she knew it beyond questioning. Joseph hadn't mentioned anything about marriage, but Emma knew it was inevitable. She just knew. But what would she do if her father never approved of that path? She couldn't bear the thought of having to choose between these two men who were so dear to her. She prayed that it would never come to such an unthinkable choice.

CHAPTER THREE

A New Family

In spite of her father's aversion to Joseph, Emma found great delight in every moment she was able to spend with him. She didn't know how their being together was possibly going to work out, but she knew that it would. They were *meant* to be together, and she felt it in her deepest self. It soon became evident when Joseph asked for her hand in marriage. Emma readily agreed, even though she knew it would take a miracle for her father to accept Joseph. Surely God would provide a way.

On a pleasant spring afternoon, Emma talked Joseph into helping her make biscuits. She got him to sing a little ditty with her, but he insisted that he would do well not to compete with her beautiful voice. While the biscuits were in the oven, the conversation became more serious. He spoke with reverence of his brother, Alvin, while he held Emma's hand.

"When he died," Joseph said, "the preacher told me that he was lost . . . because he'd never been baptized."

Sensing the depth of his sorrow—and her own aversion to the thought—she said, "You don't believe that, do you?"

Joseph shook his head. "I can't imagine God being so unmerciful. Alvin was a good man. He lived as I believe our Savior would want any man to live. It was no fault of his that the true gospel was not available to him. I don't know how it's possible, Emma, but I believe there must be another answer."

"Surely there must be. Perhaps one day you will receive an answer to that." She smiled. "I understand you're the kind of man who gets his prayers answered."

He chuckled and gave her a sidelong glance. "I just pray like any other man."

Emma wanted to tell him that he certainly was *not* like any other man. But she knew he was humble about the events that had happened in his life, and her reasons for loving him had nothing to do with his extraordinary relationship with God. She loved him for the man that he was. She longed for the day they could be married, and wondered if Joseph had read her mind when he said, "I asked your father's permission, Emma. He wouldn't even consider it."

Emma's confidence in knowing that she and Joseph were meant to be together lessened her anxiety over the situation. "Father will come around." She offered a smile that she hoped would ease *his* anxiety. "Be patient."

Weeks eased into months while Emma prayed every day and night that her father's heart would be softened—and his mind opened enough to see what a wonderful man she knew Joseph to be. Her continual pleading with her father had no effect, and she began to fear that she would be forced to make a choice that she had believed all along she could never make.

When winter came again, she wasn't surprised to hear Joseph say, "I fear we will never have your father's blessing, Emma. I don't want to get married without it, but . . . there may be no other way." He held both of her hands tightly. "We can't go on like this forever."

"I know." Emma hung her head. "I don't understand, Joseph. Why are my prayers not being heard?"

"Of course they're being heard," he said and touched her chin to tilt her face to his view. "But God cannot take away the agency of His children. If your father chooses to be this way, you can't change it—and neither can God." He chuckled in an attempt to lighten the mood. "Truthfully, if I were him, I don't know that I'd want my daughter marrying me."

"You're a good man, Joseph."

"I try to be, but . . . you and I both know I have nothing to offer a respectable lady."

"That's not true, either," she said and put a hand to his face. "So long as you always love me, and stand by me, I will never be without what matters most to me."

"You are too precious," he said, putting his hand over hers. Then his brow furrowed. "Unfortunately, your father doesn't share your sentiment . . . and I fear he never will."

"Just . . . give him a little more time."

Joseph nodded, albeit reluctantly.

Emma continued to pray with all her strength for a miracle to occur, but eventually she had to accept that what Joseph had said was true. Even God could not force the hand of His children. But her father's choice was forcing Emma into a position where she too would have to choose. There was no reason to even question what her choice might be. She knew God's will for her, and it was to be at Joseph's side, whatever that might entail. Joseph had been called to do a great work, and she had been called to fulfill her own destiny. If her greatest desire was to be a righteous woman and please God—and it was—then she had to take the path before her, however difficult it might be to go against her father's wishes. She found some comfort in knowing that her mother didn't entirely agree with his stand, but Emma knew that her mother needed to support her husband—and Emma needed to stand by the man that she knew God wanted her to marry.

With the arrival of the new year, Emma finally came to accept that sometimes life just doesn't work out the way you might have planned or hoped for. But she knew that God was with her in the decision to move forward. When it became evident that Isaac Hale's heart would not be softened, that he would never give his blessing to their marriage, Emma and Joseph were finally married without it. The marriage had not been planned, but when the opportunity presented itself, Emma took it, knowing there was no man who could fill her heart the way that Joseph did. When the time finally came, she didn't think too hard about being forced to choose between her family and Joseph. She just made her choice with full purpose of heart, trusting that God would make up the difference.

They were married on the eighteenth day of January by Squire Tarbill at his home in South Bainbridge, New York. Emma didn't mind that it was a simple, quiet affair, but she wished that her family could have been there. Still, when Joseph slid that ring on her finger and committed himself to her, she'd never felt so elated.

"Are you happy?" Joseph asked her as they left the Tarbill home.

"I am!" she said eagerly. He caught her crying a while later, but he still believed her when she insisted, "I've never been more happy."

"Nor have I," he said with typical tenderness, "but I know you're leaving much behind for me. I pray that I can make you happy, Emma . . . that I can give you a good life."

Emma smiled and put a hand to his face. "My place is with you. I've never been more sure about anything in my life. God is with us in this marriage, Joseph. We could ask for no more than that."

He smiled in return. "You're a fine woman, Mrs. Smith. And one day I will build you a fine home, and we'll have grand parties there, and I'll even dance with you."

"Is this prophecy, Mr. Smith?"

He laughed heartily. "Maybe it's just wishful thinking."

"I can live with that. Wherever we live, so long as you're there, I will be happy."

"Amen," he said and pressed a kiss into her hair.

Following their marriage, Joseph took Emma home to his family in Manchester. As they approached what he called the family's *new* home, she felt distinctly nervous. She'd heard endless tales of what a good family Joseph had come from, but she wasn't certain how they would feel about him moving in with a new bride who was not in good standing with her own family.

Joseph's parents weren't just happy to see their son, they were thrilled! Emma stood back and observed their reunion with great pleasure. Then he turned, and Emma saw the affection he felt for her and his pride in introducing her to his family.

"Oh, my dear!" Lucy Smith said with a beaming smile and perfect acceptance. "How wonderful to have you here!" She immediately embraced Emma with a tightness that echoed the sincerity of her greeting. Emma found herself close to tears as a comforting peace soothed her empty ache in thinking of her own mother.

"Thank you," was all that Emma could think to say.

Lucy eased back and took hold of Emma's shoulders, saying, "Oh, she's precious, Joseph!"

"She is, indeed." Joseph beamed, and his mother moved aside to allow Joseph's father to greet his new daughter-in-law. Emma knew that his name was also Joseph.

Father Smith took both of Emma's hands into his and gave her a bright smile that caused him to resemble his son. "It's so good to meet you. Come, let's get you warmed up."

"And you must be hungry," Lucy added.

"Thank you," Emma said again, then observed as Joseph greeted each of his younger brothers and sisters with enthusiasm.

Sophronia was near Emma's age, and immediately treated Emma as if they had been sisters all of their lives. Samuel was a little younger than Joseph, followed by William, then Katharine, who was near the age Joseph had been when he'd encountered his first vision. Don Carlos was a few years younger than Katharine, and Little Lucy was the youngest, and still a child. Emma learned that while each of the children officially lived at home, the older ones often left home for periods of time to find work. They were all kind and gracious toward Emma, and she could see that all he'd told her was true; they were a good family with deep ties. Thinking of Joseph's visions and the accompanying trials, she could see evidence that the support his family had given him through both had strengthened their bonds.

They'd been there about an hour when Emma thought she might finally get warm again following their winter journey. Aware that Lucy was working on supper preparations, she was about to offer her help when she heard the front door open and close, and a man's voice say with joyful fervor, "Where is she?"

Emma heard Joseph laugh and turned to see him embracing a man near his own height. "It's good to see you, Hyrum," Joseph said as he stepped back and took his brother's shoulders into his hands.

As their eyes met, Emma could almost see a tangible connection there. "It's been way too long, little brother," Hyrum said. They both laughed and again shared a brotherly embrace.

Joseph then turned toward Emma, and she felt warmed to see at least equal adoration toward her as that he had shown for his brother. "This is Emma," Joseph said as if he were announcing royalty, holding out a hand toward her.

Hyrum turned to look at her, his eyes sparkling with intrigue. Without words he said, *So this is the woman who captured my brother's heart.* Was he also wondering if she was woman enough to stand beside a man with such a great and sacred calling? Her own moment of self-doubt was washed away by the overt admiration in this man's countenance. Joseph added with tender pride, "Emma, this is my dear brother, Hyrum."

Hyrum stepped forward eagerly and wrapped both his hands around one of Emma's. "It is truly a pleasure, Mrs. Smith."

"The pleasure is mine," Emma said. "I've heard more good about you than I could ever recount."

Hyrum tossed his brother a scowl that was both comical and skeptical, and Joseph chuckled. Emma's eyes were drawn past Hyrum's shoulder the same moment as he turned and motioned toward the woman that Emma just now realized had come in with him. "My wife, Jerusha," he said with the same tenderness in his voice that Emma had heard in Joseph's when he'd introduced *her.*

"Oh, my sister!" Jerusha said and eased past her husband to embrace Emma tightly. The word *sister* captured Emma as surely as the warmth in Jerusha's hug. Thoughts of her own sisters stung her eyes, but missing them was soothed by the sweetness surrounding her.

Settling into life as a member of the Smith family was much easier for Emma than she'd anticipated. She truly found compensation for leaving her family behind by the way she was taken in so warmly by Joseph's. It took little time to discover for herself that all Joseph had told her of the goodness of his family had still not prepared her for their kindness. Hyrum and Jerusha lived just down the road, and Emma quickly grew close to both of them, seeing continual evidence that all Joseph had told her of his dear brother—and more—was true. Their closeness as brothers touched Emma, and she enjoyed seeing them together, whether at work or in conversations over spiritual matters. Both Hyrum and his wife truly treated her as a sister, as did Joseph's other siblings. The support of Joseph's family in his endeavors was continually evident. They loved him and believed in him, and that gave them all something wonderful in common.

While the men spent their days working out in the cold, Emma quickly felt at home helping in the kitchen and around the house. She and Lucy had much to talk about. Emma was surprised at how easily she was able to share with her new mother-in-law the tender feelings of her heart regarding her father's attitude toward Joseph, and how difficult it had been to be forced to choose. But she made it clear that she knew she'd made the right choice, and she felt no qualms or regret. Lucy was kind and compassionate over the matter, as she was with everything. She also shared experiences of her own life that Emma enjoyed hearing. And she loved to hear the stories of Joseph's childhood from his mother's perspective. When Emma asked about Joseph's illness that had resulted in the need for that excruciatingly painful surgery on his leg, Lucy stopped working and sat down at the table to talk about it. Even after all these years, Lucy became emotional when speaking of Joseph's pain, and Emma realized that from the perspective of a mother, witnessing a child's suffering was likely more difficult than personally enduring it.

"He was so brave," Lucy said, using the corner of her apron to dab at her eyes. "He told his father that he didn't want me to have to watch." She paused briefly, and more tears came. "Even at such a tender age—and in such pain—he was more concerned for me than for himself." She smiled. "He's still that way." Lucy sighed, her eyes distant. "The doctors wanted to take his leg. I wouldn't let them do it. I just felt that it was wrong. There were moments when I doubted my decision, but with time I came to know that it was right." She laughed gently. "Well, to see him now is evidence of that."

"It is indeed," Emma said, and they were soon back to work.

While Lucy kneaded bread and Emma scrubbed carrots from the cellar, preparing them to go into a stew, they continued to chat comfortably. A lull came in their conversation, then Lucy said, "I can't help wondering, my dear . . . what did you think . . . when he told you? About the visions?"

Emma clearly recalled that day, and how she had felt regarding Joseph's confessions. "From the first," she said, "I just knew . . . that he was telling the truth."

Lucy smiled, not seeming at all surprised, then her eyes became thoughtful. "His brothers were like that," she said. When her expression saddened, Emma didn't even have to wonder where her thoughts were.

"It must have been so difficult losing Alvin," she said.

Lucy looked surprised by the comment, then not so surprised. "It was, yes," she said, pausing in her work. "It was difficult for all of us. In truth, even now we have difficulty speaking of it." Lucy struggled for composure. "He and Joseph were especially close." She leaned a little closer. "The angel Moroni told Joseph that Alvin was to accompany him when the time came to finally receive the plates."

Emma reflected on the way Lucy so matter-of-factly discussed such miraculous goings-on, then she considered what Lucy's last statement meant. "Then who *will* accompany him . . . when the time comes?"

"If Joseph knows, he's not said. But it will surely be the Lord's choice, not his."

"Certainly," Emma said, logically assuming that it would likely be Hyrum.

Emma felt deeply grateful for the love and acceptance she received from Joseph's parents, and for the example they set in the love and respect they shared. Lucy confided to Emma that they had always had a difference of opinion concerning organized religion, and it was Lucy's fondest hope that one day they would be united in their beliefs. Lucy felt sure that eventually her prayers would be answered. Emma had to agree. Such gentle conversations became common between Emma and Lucy, and Emma felt inclined to believe that the quiet kinship they shared would be a great sustaining factor in her life.

For Emma, that first summer of her marriage to Joseph was akin to heaven. They both worked very hard with the family in order to see that needs were met, and their involvement in all that the family did was fulfilling in many ways. Joseph and Emma talked often of their future, their dreams, and their deepest feelings. Emma often heard her husband speculating over how their lives might unfold in relation to what God might require of him. It was evident that for all he had seen and been taught, he still had little idea of what to expect. But he was a man of great faith, determined to take each step the Lord asked him to take, trusting that the next step would show itself at the right time. In light of Joseph's mission, Emma knew that many facets of their future were difficult to plan. But they still talked of having a home of their own and many children. They both wanted a large family, and they looked forward to the day when their first child might arrive.

Emma felt safe and secure and perfectly happy in her new life. Joseph treated her like a queen, and she couldn't imagine being more blessed. Especially close to Emma's heart was the day that Joseph took her to the place where he had witnessed that most miraculous vision. They ambled slowly through the woods until he came to a certain place and reverently declared that this was the place it had happened. He gazed upward through the trees, nostalgia glowing in his eyes, and she could well imagine the clarity of his memory. His voice lowered in reverence. "I saw Their faces." He sighed. "I heard Them speak. They knew me . . . by name."

Emma felt a chill rush over her shoulders, accompanied by a warmth in her heart that confirmed to her once again the truthfulness of his declaration. She looked up into the treetops herself, unable to comprehend such a remarkable vision. But through Joseph's prior descriptions, it was not so difficult to imagine. Even if she could never fully comprehend what it must have been like to be in the presence of divine beings, her awe was beyond words. They stood there together in silence for long minutes, their hands clasped. She saw him close his eyes, and gathered that he was likely recounting the memory to himself in vivid detail. He surely drew strength from his absolute knowledge that it had been real. Emma took advantage of the quiet to consider the reality that she was married to a prophet, a man who had seen God—face-to-face; a man chosen to do a great mission. She felt certain that as he fully embarked upon that mission, the simple nature of their life together would change. A different kind of chill rushed over her, as if warning her to be prepared for great difficulties to come, and because of this, she put more effort into absorbing the present moment into her spirit. The knowledge of what had happened in this very spot would sustain them both.

Just a few days later, Emma sat on a fence with Jerusha beside her, both cheering for their husbands as they ran past. Emma thought of Lucy telling her how she'd stood up to the doctors who had wanted to remove Joseph's leg. His ability to run like that now was a miracle.

Following the race, the four of them enjoyed a picnic while the men bantered with good-natured humor.

"I let you win," Joseph declared.

"I'm sure," Hyrum said with light sarcasm.

When they were all walking toward home, Emma and Jerusha ambled side by side, talking about a cookie recipe, while the men walked a few paces behind, discussing the work they'd been doing alongside their father. Then Emma heard Hyrum say to his brother, "It won't be long now . . . until you're to obtain the record."

"No, not much longer," Joseph replied, while she and Jerusha exchanged a knowing glance. All of Joseph's family was well aware of the situation, but to Emma it still felt strange at times to hear them speak of it no differently than if they were discussing the building of fences or what they might have for supper.

"Has the Lord revealed who is meant to go with you," Hyrum asked, "now that Alvin is gone?" The tone of his voice made clear what Lucy had told Emma; they had difficulty even speaking of anything to do with Alvin's absence.

"Yes," Joseph answered, and Emma listened with anticipation to see who it would be. But Joseph turned the conversation to speculation over what might take place once the record was in his possession. With all the heckling the family had gotten over the hidden gold Bible, the men both agreed they needed to be very careful.

"Perhaps it's good that you're living here with family at this time," Hyrum said.

"I'm absolutely certain of it," Joseph agreed firmly. "What would we ever do without family?"

Emma glanced over her shoulder, and Joseph smiled at her, then he caught up a few steps and took her hand. Later that night, while their heads were close together on the same pillow, they talked of what a lovely day they'd had, and they counted blessings. When it became silent, she wondered if he was drifting into sleep until he said, "Emma . . . the Lord has revealed to me who is to go with me to get the plates."

"You mentioned that earlier."

"It's you, Emma."

"Me?" She gasped and leaned up on one elbow, needing to see Joseph's face to be sure he meant it. When she couldn't see it in the darkness, she lit the candle on the bedside table, then turned toward him. "Me?" she repeated.

"Yes," he said, and she saw the truth of it in his eyes even before he added, "You need to know, Emma, it's not just a matter of my personal preference—although it certainly *would* be. You are *the Lord's* choice. I must go up the hill to get the plates alone, but I need you close by; I need you to wait for me."

"I will!" she said eagerly.

"We must be careful, Emma." He took her hand. "I've been warned to protect them . . . and you've heard the ridiculous notions that people around here have gotten."

"Are you worried?"

"A little, yes . . . but I must trust in the Lord to help us. I'm certain everything will be fine."

For many days Emma pondered what it meant for her husband to have the sacred record entrusted to his hands. She felt privileged and humbled to think that she was the one meant to go with him on this solemn errand, that he needed her near while he took care of the matter. Emma loved to hear him talk about his prior visits with the Angel Moroni. She could see a light glowing in his eyes that seemed a reflection of the glory he had witnessed, and she couldn't help but share his zeal for the wondrous work that was about to commence. What must it be like, she wondered, to be in the presence of angels? She couldn't even imagine, but she never doubted that Joseph's reports were true.

When the appointed night arrived, Emma felt a combination of excitement and fear. There had been much talk and speculation in the community over Joseph obtaining the record, and many rumors had come to their ears that others might try to steal the plates due to their being reputedly made of gold. Joseph had been warned that protecting the plates was of the utmost importance, and Emma shared her husband's concern that doing so might not be easy. But they prayed together that all would be well, and she believed that it surely would be.

They left the house together after everyone but Lucy had retired, taking with them a horse and wagon that belonged to Mr. Knight, a good friend of Joseph's. He was the same man Joseph had stayed with while he and Emma had been courting, and he'd loaned Joseph his cutter to come and visit her. Joseph had confided in Mr. Knight regarding his experiences, and he knew that the time had come for the record to be put into Joseph's care. Hence, the timing of his visit was surely not coincidence. He'd brought with him a Mr. Stowell, who was also a friend to Joseph; both men were very supportive of his work. It was Mr. Stowell whom Joseph had been working for when he had first come to Pennsylvania and met Emma.

Joseph helped Emma up onto the seat of the wagon and sat beside her. He snapped the reins, and the horse moved along. Joseph didn't have much to say during the course of the drive, and Emma felt sure he was deep in contemplation over what might transpire this night. And he was surely recalling his previous encounters with the angel. Emma allowed him the silence to do his pondering, while her own thoughts tumbled. She wished she had any idea what to expect as he guided the wagon deeper into the woods. When he drew back on the reins to halt, her heart began to pound. He guided the reins into her hands, then pressed his own hands around hers for a long moment.

"I don't know how long I'll be," he said.

She nodded with firmness, silently encouraging him to do whatever needed to be done. "I'll be fine," she said with a confident smile. She didn't want him to be distracted with any concern for her. He smiled back and pressed a quick but sincere kiss to her cheek, then he jumped down and disappeared before she could draw another breath.

Emma didn't know how long Joseph was gone before her heart began to settle. For a long while she just sat and waited, her mind wandering aimlessly. Then it suddenly occurred to her that her husband was surely conversing with an angel. Something warm inside her—subtle but undeniable—confirmed the truth of her thoughts.

A noise from the darkened woods startled her, and she gasped. Had she imagined it, or was it possible that someone or something was out there? Only silence answered her question, and she scolded herself for being so anxious. She felt cold and wrapped her cloak more tightly around her. The horse twitched and snorted, then settled. As her thoughts wandered, her nervousness heightened. Was Joseph all right? What could be taking so long? Had someone followed him with the intent to do him harm?

Fighting the fear that tightened her heart, Emma closed her eyes and prayed that her husband would be kept safe, and his errand would take place without incident. She reminded herself that this was the Lord's errand, and surely Joseph *would* be protected. She occupied her mind with thoughts of Joseph's visions and her own feelings that had confirmed their truthfulness.

Time dragged on while her thoughts and feelings vacillated back and forth between faith and fear, hope and trepidation. Every little noise put her on edge, especially when the horse twitched or snorted. The cold settled into her more deeply while she lost any sense of the hours passing; she only knew that the night was wearing on, and she had to believe that everything was all right. She got down from the wagon to ease the stiffness in her back; she talked quietly to the horse and stroked it gently, as if doing so might ease her own anxiety. She longed to sleep, tired from a long day, but felt she should remain awake and alert. She climbed back onto the seat of the wagon, certain that when Joseph *did* return, they would need to leave quickly.

Emma was startled to realize that dawn was approaching as the trees surrounding her became slowly more visible. And in the predawn light, Joseph finally appeared. She heaved a sigh of immeasurable relief just to see him. She considered what heavenly tutelage might have been taking place all through the night, then noticed the heavy bundle he carried, wrapped in his coat. He was out of breath as if he'd been running, and she wondered if he had some sense of someone following him. But she didn't ask, and he said little as he put the bundle into the back of the wagon. The way he groaned as he lifted the plates let her know that they were heavy. She wondered what they looked like, felt like. She also considered what a miracle it was that he *could* run, considering his childhood trauma. Surely God had foreseen this day in Joseph's life.

He climbed onto the seat beside her, kissed her cheek in greeting, and took the reins. While he drove, he repeated some of the instructions he'd been given, and the concerns he had about what might be required to accomplish all that he'd been commissioned to do. But his confidence in himself was strengthened by his knowledge that God would be with them both as they pressed forward. Emma was overcome with a deep thrill to hear Joseph recount his experience. She also felt an overwhelming sense of privilege to be here with him, and to be the first to hear what had occurred.

They stopped again, and Emma waited while Joseph went into the woods to hide the record. Again she was made aware of the cumbersome weight of the plates by the effort it took for him to lift and carry them, still wrapped in his coat. He was gone for some time while Emma fought the desire for sleep, reminding herself that Joseph had to be equally tired.

Emma was grateful to return home, as she knew Joseph was. When they walked into the house, Lucy's expression was enough to let them know she had been terribly worried.

"Oh, you're all right!" she said.

"Yes, Mother," Joseph assured her, "everything is fine."

Breakfast was over, but Lucy made certain they had something to eat, then she insisted they get some rest. Joseph didn't rest long, however, before he went out to help his father. Emma rested just a while longer before she sought out Lucy to see what she might do to help in the house. Emma pondered the events of the previous night throughout the remainder of the day as she went about her work. She considered it truly amazing that this humble family would be at the center of such miracles! And she could only feel privileged to be among them.

CHAPTER FOUR

Treasure

It was a stormy night when Joseph went to retrieve the plates from where he'd hidden them in the woods. Emma could hardly keep herself from pacing the floor while he was gone, but she did her best to appear calm, not wanting others in the family to be alarmed. How could she not think of the men who might be out there, watching for him to leave the house to get this so-called treasure? She knew the kind of men they were; she'd been with Joseph numerous times when such men had stopped them on the streets, publicly harassing him with talk of getting their hands on the gold. She found it ironic that while they heckled Joseph and persecuted him concerning his visions, proclaiming derisively that they were surely nonsense and had no merit, there was still a general belief that he did indeed have some great treasure in his possession. She was often tempted to point out this contradiction in their perception of the situation, but she thought it best to keep such thoughts to herself.

When Joseph finally returned, wet from rain and out of breath, Emma's relief at seeing that he was fine only lasted a moment.

"I was pursued in the woods," he reported to the family members present, "and attacked."

"Are you all right?" Emma demanded. "Did they hurt you?"

"I'm fine," he assured her.

"What did you do?" his brother asked.

"I fought back, of course. I hit one of them with the plates."

"What?" Emma gasped. "You can barely lift them!"

"I managed this time."

"Was he hurt?" Lucy asked.

"I assume," Joseph said. "But it was either me or him. I must protect the plates."

Emma knew that was true, and she prayed very hard that the Lord would protect *him* while he had them in his care. She had a feeling this was only the beginning of such troubles.

It quickly became evident that Joseph's charge regarding the protection of the plates would not be easy. Public harassment continued over the rumors of his supposedly having treasure in his possession. But far worse, the Smith home was actually invaded more than once by ruffians intent on acquiring this gold artifact for personal gain. Emma was appalled at how greed could provoke men to such behavior. At times she felt utterly afraid on behalf of herself, as well as Joseph and every member of his family. Then she would remind herself that the matter was in God's hands, and they would all surely be protected as they did their best to protect the plates.

Emma seldom had any idea where Joseph kept the plates hidden, for they were rarely in the same place for long. And even though he sometimes called on family members to help hide them, they always remained concealed in a wooden box that had belonged to Alvin. Moroni had made it clear that for the time being, only Joseph would be allowed to actually see them. And all those committed to helping him respected that charge.

The situation became so challenging that Joseph and Emma discussed the matter and knew they had no choice but to leave.

If the presence of the plates was putting his home and family in danger, then Joseph felt he needed to take the plates elsewhere, to a place where people would be oblivious to anything out of the ordinary taking place.

"I agree that we need to leave," Emma said to her husband, holding his hand in the dark while he lay close beside her, "but how will we manage?"

"I don't know," Joseph said with heaviness in his voice. "At least we have a place to go," he said. "I consider that a miracle."

Emma agreed with him. Her faith had been strengthened when her own father's heart was softened over news of their troubles, and he agreed to let her and Joseph return to Harmony and stay in her parents' home. And her brother Alva would be coming more than 150 miles with his wagon to help them move. To Emma this was not simply an answer to prayers; it was a *miracle,* just as Joseph had said. Emma's Pennsylvania home was dear to her, and she longed for the company of her family. She felt certain that if her father only had the opportunity to get to know Joseph as she did, his heart would be softened even further.

"Still, we have no money to speak of," she said, unable to help feeling concerned.

She heard Joseph sigh with the weight of the problem, and a moment later he said with firmness, "We must trust in the Lord, Emma. If our purpose for leaving is to protect the plates that He has entrusted to me, then surely He will provide us the means to do so."

"I suppose I should have more faith," she said.

Joseph chuckled and turned more toward her. "I believe you have a great deal of faith, Mrs. Smith. After all . . . you married me—a man with nothing to his name."

"That wasn't faith, Joseph," she said, chuckling as well. "That was love."

More seriously he said, "And what was it that made you believe I had seen visions and angels, Emma? What has made you willing to stand by me when my life is surrounded by strangeness?"

He touched her face with tenderness, and she touched his in return. "It's not so difficult to believe in something when you know in your heart that it's true."

He chuckled again. "I think they call that faith."

Emma snuggled close to him and whispered, "It will be difficult to leave, Joseph. Your family has been so good to me."

"They love you," he said as if it were nothing. "I love you as well."

"And they love *you;* that's evident." She sighed. "In spite of the danger, I feel safe with them . . . with your father and brothers around."

"Yes," Joseph said with distinct sadness, "it will be difficult to leave."

Emma drifted to sleep in his arms and woke up praying that she could have sufficient faith to leave the care and protection of Joseph's family and embark on a new journey at her husband's side.

Once again Emma was humbled by her husband's faith when a man named Martin Harris, a neighbor and friend of Joseph's, insisted on giving them fifty dollars to help meet their needs. Joseph offered to sign a note to agree to pay it back, but Martin insisted that it was his way of furthering the cause that Joseph was engaged in. Emma's gratitude was deep. Without Mr. Harris's kindness, she wondered what they might have done.

When Emma's brother Alva arrived with his wagon, Emma ran out to greet him, and Joseph followed. Alva tied the reins off and jumped down, laughing as he hugged Emma tightly, lifting her off the ground. After he'd set his sister down, he turned and held out a hand to Joseph, who shook it heartily. "It's good to see you again, Alva," he said. "We can't thank you enough for your help."

"Anything for my sister," he said, winking at Emma. Joseph smiled at his wife, and they took Alva inside to introduce him to the family and get him something to eat.

Early the following morning, Alva's wagon was taken into the barn to be loaded with Joseph and Emma's few belongings. Emma watched as Hyrum and Alva helped Joseph situate an empty barrel in the wagon. The wooden box containing the plates was then lowered in.

"Whoa, they're heavy," Alva commented, watching Joseph lift them with effort over the edge of the barrel, then set them carefully at the bottom. Beans were poured in over the box, burying the precious record deeply inside.

When everything was loaded, they could no longer put off difficult good-byes. Emma had perfect empathy for how hard it was for Joseph to part with each member of his family. She knew he was especially struggling over having to take leave of his parents and Hyrum. Emma shared his sentiments. She'd grown close to Joseph's family and loved them dearly.

Once they were on their way, Emma focused on what lay ahead, rather than on what they were leaving behind. Her sorrow at leaving was compensated by knowing that she would be reunited with her own family. But she knew that Joseph could not, in all practicality, share her enthusiasm. Her father's feelings about him were no secret, and Emma prayed that their living under the same roof would go well.

While she sat between her husband and her brother, the three of them sharing pleasant conversation, Emma thought of the plates hidden in the barrel. She wanted to think that such a precaution wasn't necessary, but she wasn't at all surprised when they were stopped and their belongings searched. The assailants didn't bother searching too deeply into the barrel when all they found were beans, and the plates were left undetected.

Once on their way again, Alva commented, "So, this kind of thing happens often, does it?"

"I'm afraid it does," Joseph said and put his arm around Emma's shoulders, discreetly pressing a kiss into her hair, as if to silently apologize for its effect on her. She took his hand and squeezed it.

Emma wondered what her brother might be thinking about all this, and what Joseph might tell him. So far the issue hadn't been discussed beyond the necessity to keep the plates hidden. She wasn't at all surprised when Alva said, "So, tell me about these plates—as you call them. I'd like to hear *your* version, Joseph."

Emma was thrilled to hear the story once again. The warmth she felt inside reaffirmed the truth of what Joseph was saying, and Alva's genuine interest gave her hope that other members of her family might now be more receptive to Joseph's mission.

The long journey was rewarded when Emma's home came into view.

"You know, Alva," Joseph said, pointing at the house, "this is where I first met the woman who captured my heart."

Alva went along. "Do I know her?"

"Not likely." Joseph winked at Emma. "But I'll warn you, she's mighty tough to come up against in fishing . . . or a horse race."

"And don't you forget it," Emma said, then laughed, taking hold of Joseph's arm.

The moment Alva brought the wagon to a stop, Emma's mother came out the door. Joseph helped Emma step down, and the two women shared an embrace laced with tears and laughter. Emma then turned to see her father, who opened his arms and smiled. Her tears increased as she felt his familiar grasp that took her back to her childhood.

"Hello, Father," she said, smiling at him as she wiped her tears.

"It's good to have you back," he said, and her heart swelled with hope that their past differences would be permanently erased.

Her heart quickened with a combination of hope and dread as Joseph approached Isaac Hale, his hand outstretched. "It's good to see you again, Mr. Hale," Joseph said brightly. "We're very grateful for your allowing us to stay."

Isaac took the proffered handshake, and Emma breathed a deep sigh of relief. "Let's get this wagon unloaded, shall we?" Isaac said kindly.

Emma felt indescribably happy to be in the kitchen with her mother again, helping her prepare supper, chatting as if they'd never been apart—except that there was so much to catch up on. Elizabeth was thrilled to hear that Joseph had such a fine family, and that they'd been so kind to Emma. And she was even more thrilled to have her daughter back.

At the supper table, Emma was glad to hear her father making polite conversation with Joseph, until he said, "I understand you were having some trouble in New York."

"Yes, sir," Joseph said, "we certainly were. We are truly grateful to be here now, and for your hospitality."

"What kind of trouble?" Isaac asked.

Emma answered, "Many people have completely misunderstood what Joseph is doing, Father. Some have heard rumors that he has the ancient record . . . and it's written on plates of gold. There are men who have tried to steal the plates."

Isaac looked straight at Joseph and asked, *"Do* you have these reputed gold plates?"

Joseph exchanged a cautious glance with Emma before he said firmly, "Yes, sir. I do."

"I would very much like to see them," Isaac said, his tone indicating that he didn't believe they truly existed.

"Father," Emma said, "it's—"

Joseph stopped Emma by taking her hand beneath the table. "I'm afraid that's not possible," he said to his father-in-law without apology. Isaac looked disgruntled, but Emma's mother gracefully steered the conversation elsewhere.

Not many days later, Joseph graciously attempted to appease Isaac's concerns without going against what he'd been instructed to do. He allowed Isaac to hold the box containing the plates, so that he could feel their immense weight and realize that something significant was surely inside. Isaac seemed temporarily satisfied, but with the passing of a few more days, he once again asked to see them, insisting that he wasn't going to be kept in the dark concerning something like this in his own home.

Joseph was kind and respectful as he said, "The Lord has made it clear that I'm to show the record to no one."

Isaac stared at Joseph as if he truly believed him to be mad. He echoed with disbelief, *"The Lord?"*

"Yes, sir," Joseph said.

Emma's mother once again gracefully steered the conversation elsewhere, but the strain at the supper table remained. That night, alone in their room, Emma suggested to her husband, "Perhaps it would be best not to be so bold in your declarations in speaking to my father."

"I simply stated a fact, Emma. I can't lie to him or to anyone else."

"I know that, but . . ."

"Emma," he took her hand, "how can your father accept me for who and what I am if he doesn't know what that is? I can't change what the Lord has asked me to do . . . or be ashamed to speak of it."

Emma sighed and looked down. "I know," she said. "You're right. I just . . . want him to be proud of you." She looked up and touched his face. "The way I'm proud of you."

"I don't know if that will ever be," he said. "I only wish that his feelings for me did not reflect upon you. I want him to be proud of *you,* Emma. You're his daughter."

Emma wanted that too, but she changed the conversation as gracefully as her mother had earlier. She wondered if her father would *ever* be proud of her again.

Emma prayed night and day that her father's heart would be softened toward her husband, but once Isaac realized that Joseph would not back down on allowing him to see the plates, he insisted that Joseph was not welcome in his home. Isaac believed that his son-in-law was a dreamer and a fool, and that Emma was a fool for believing in him.

Once again Joseph and Emma were confronted with having to move, and once again a solution presented itself. Considering the scarcely polite tolerance that Isaac Hale had for Joseph, it seemed a good decision for them to live across the road. The structure was actually a shed that had once been used to tan hides, but Emma did her best to make it a home for her and Joseph, and she was grateful. Living close to her parents gave Emma hope that the tension between them could be rectified. Surely with more time and the opportunity for her father to see firsthand what a good man Joseph was, and how well he treated her, his heart would be softened toward him. Her hopes were strengthened when her father agreed to sell Joseph a portion of his land.

As tiny and rugged as their little home was, Emma loved being there with Joseph. And she was understandably excited when he was able to finally begin the work of translation. At the supper table one evening, Joseph complimented her on the meal, then said, "I need you to write for me, Emma . . . while I translate."

"Like . . . a scribe?"

"Yes, that's it."

"But I'm not supposed to see the plates."

"That's not so difficult to figure out," he said. "We'll start tomorrow . . . if that's all right."

"Yes, certainly," she said, inwardly thrilled with the prospect of being actively involved in his work. She could hardly sleep that night as she considered what treasured things might be locked away in these ancient records preserved and protected by angels.

The following morning after breakfast, the dictation began, and Emma wrote what Joseph said, even though she couldn't see the plates. He was very careful to heed the admonition of the Angel Moroni that no one was to see them unless commanded by the Lord. Emma was determined to honor such a critical policy with exactness, not wanting to do anything that might thwart Joseph's work.

When they first began, Emma waited, almost breathless, to hear what he might say. As the work progressed, she was continually in awe of how the words would flow so smoothly from Joseph's mouth. Intricate stories unraveled with the same ease as profound doctrines that came forth in near-perfect form. Even when they would take a break, he would come back to it and not miss a word, without having to ask her where they had left off. Emma felt a continual awareness of the miracle that was taking place, especially based on the level of education she knew her husband possessed. It would simply be impossible for a man to do what he was doing by any other means than divine intervention.

Emma's joy in seeing the miracle unfold was dampened when her father made a point of declaring his feelings to her. "How exactly does your husband intend to make a living for his family? He does nothing that I can see. I can't even imagine how you're getting by."

"Joseph must do as the Lord has commanded, Father; he must translate the record. He must commit himself to it fully." Her father made a scoffing noise, but she ignored it and turned to gentle pleading. "Father, if you would just . . . consider the possibility that what Joseph is doing is of God, I'm certain that—"

"I don't want to hear another word about it. I'm not the kind of man to be taken in by such madness. And I'm concerned about my daughter's welfare."

"There's no need," she said with firmness. "Joseph is very good to me, and the Lord will provide our needs."

Isaac let out a cynical noise that pricked Emma. "You're married to a fool, Emma," he growled with a combination of disappointment and disgust. "If he can't settle down and let go of these ridiculous notions, I'll not have him in my house."

Emma swallowed carefully, determined to keep a steady voice. "If you believe your threats will make him change his mind about what he's doing, Father, it will never happen. He knows that what he's doing is right—and I know it, too."

Isaac shook his head, as if her words were pitiful. "As I've told you before, if you believe that, Emma, you're as big a fool as he is."

Emma walked away, which was her only option other than bursting into tears in front of her father. She managed to hold them back until she was outside, and she didn't fully let them loose until she'd crossed the road and was alone in her own little home. She tried to tell herself that her father's opinions didn't matter, but they did. She would never be swayed from knowing what was true and right, but her father's disdain hurt her deeply.

Joseph found her crying and held her close until she had fully vented every tear. "What is it?" he asked with typical tenderness.

"Oh, I bet you could never guess," she said with mild sarcasm as she sniffled loudly.

"Ah, your father believes your husband is a fool."

Emma sniffled again, trying to lighten the mood for Joseph's sake, if not her own. "You're very insightful, Mr. Smith. Perhaps the Lord has recognized that quality in you; maybe that's why you were chosen."

"Perhaps," he drawled with a big smile, "the Lord gave me a very insightful wife." He kissed her brow and wiped her cheeks with his fingers. "I love you, Emma. I'm sorry this is so difficult for you."

"There's no reason for you to apologize, Joseph. I still pray that my father will come around."

"I pray for that too."

Emma smiled and kissed him, then she coerced him into helping her fix supper. She gave him some carrots to scrub and cut while she did the same with the potatoes. Working together at the table, she said, "There's something I need to tell you, Joseph."

He lifted his eyes and stopped working. "Yes?"

Emma couldn't hold back a little burst of laughter, which she felt sure gave her secret away even before she said, "We're going to have a baby."

"Really?" Joseph laughed joyfully, and she nodded. He laughed again and pushed his chair back, going to his knees in front of her. "Oh, that's wonderful, Emma!" He took her face into his hands. "Are you all right? Is everything—"

"I'm fine," she insisted and wrapped her arms around him. "Everything is perfect."

"So it is," he said, and Emma couldn't deny that it was. All things considered, they had much to be grateful for, and she was truly happy.

The translation of the record continued, and somehow they were always able to get by. Emma enjoyed every minute she was able to work as Joseph's scribe. She loved to hear the stories unfold, and was always filled with anticipation over what profound spiritual principle might be in the next sentence. Between stretches of translating, she and Joseph often discussed the glorious treasure contained in the words that were coming forth. They heartily agreed that the value of gold that comprised the actual plates was surely insignificant in contrast to the priceless words that had been kept prisoner on their pages for centuries.

Emma wanted to help Joseph every waking minute, but as the effects of her pregnancy became difficult to contend with, she couldn't keep up with the tasks necessary to maintain their household and still give Joseph the help he needed. Not wanting to slow down the work, they were both grateful when her brother Alva was able to assist him. His interest and support were a pleasant blessing.

Emma was keenly aware of the baby inside of her growing and coming to life, all the while marveling at the wondrous work that was taking place beneath her own roof. And they were continually blessed with evidence that the Lord would provide all that they needed in order to move forward. Joseph's friend Martin Harris came to visit, wanting to help in any way that he could. Emma liked Martin, and appreciated his belief in Joseph and his work. He helped with the translation and was very supportive.

In spite of Emma's ongoing wish that her father would approve of Joseph's work, she loved being near her family. Having her mother close by was truly a blessing, especially as Emma anticipated the birth of her first baby. Nothing could make Emma happier than to have a child; *Joseph's* child. The miracle of creating life together was surely the greatest manifestation of the love they shared. And they *did* love each other—more every day. At the time she'd married Joseph, she could not have imagined loving him any more than she did then. But each day her warmth toward him, and their dependence on each other, grew and deepened. Not only did she love him, but he was the truest and best friend she'd ever had. She often wondered how she had ever lived without him, and prayed that she would never have to. She believed that she could face almost anything, so long as Joseph was by her side. And now they would be having a baby together. Anticipation of the event filled Emma with a continual joy that compensated for other challenges in their lives.

Emma pondered the passing of time when she noted that the air held only a hint of winter's chill as the oncoming spring fought to overtake it. That evening she sat on the edge of the bed to brush out her hair, and a moment later she found Joseph beside her, taking the brush from her hand. Long after her hair was free of every tangle, they sat close together, holding hands and speculating over the forthcoming birth of their first child, and the joy they would share in being parents.

As Emma's pregnancy progressed, Joseph became troubled by Martin Harris's request to borrow the manuscript pages of what had been translated thus far, so that he could take them to Palmyra to show his wife and ease her concerns. Apparently she had no intention of supporting her husband in *his* support of Joseph if she could not see evidence of the work for herself. Joseph told Emma that he'd gone to the Lord with Martin's request, and he had clearly been told no. But Martin persisted, and Joseph asked the Lord again. Joseph discussed the matter at length with Emma, and she shared his frustration over this dilemma. Even though her experiences with Mrs. Harris had not been positive, Emma could understand a woman's desire to have some evidence of her husband's endeavors. Martin had done much to help Joseph. Still, the Lord had said no. Twice.

Emma was surprised when Joseph told her he'd gone to the Lord a third time to ask on Martin's behalf, and this time consent had been given. She felt concerned for reasons that were difficult to define. She knew Joseph shared her concern, but Martin promised to take good care of the 116 pages that were entrusted to his care.

"I only hope," Emma said to Joseph after they'd watched Martin walk away with his precious bundle, "that he understands what treasure he has in his possession."

"Yes, so do I," Joseph said with an edge of worry in his voice.

The day after Martin left for Palmyra with the translated pages, Emma was startled by a sudden pain. As both hands went to her lower belly, she gasped and attempted to accept that it was time. She wondered if every woman was struck with this unsettling mixture of fear and hope at the onset of labor with a first child. As the pain let up, she took a moment to steady her breathing before she sat down and waited, wondering what might happen next. She'd never done this before, but she did know that the pains were meant to come at regular intervals. She lost track of minutes passing while her mind whirled with mixed thoughts. And then it happened again. That's when she called, "Joseph!"

He was at her side within a moment. "What is it?" he asked, alarmed by the urgency in her voice.

"It's time," she said with an effort to smile.

"Oh!" he muttered and made Emma laugh by his flustered attempt to figure out what to do next. He helped her to bed and made certain she was comfortable before he ran across the road to get her mother, and then he went for the midwife. They had discussed this and planned carefully, but as the pain progressed, Emma was shocked by its intensity. Her gratitude for having her mother with her went beyond words. The hours that followed forced her to humbly accept that for all of her being warned by other women of how difficult this would be, she'd been wholly unprepared. Never had she comprehended such pain! As the time drew near and the fierceness of her suffering only worsened, she found it ironic that she longed for this cup to pass from her, and immediately the Savior's example replaced the thought. *Nevertheless, not my will, but thine be done.*

When her little boy was finally delivered, Emma had never felt such relief and joy. "Alvin," she whispered as he was placed in her arms. It was the name she and Joseph had chosen. No greater treasure had ever been bestowed upon her than that of her newborn son; Joseph's son. *Their* son.

CHAPTER FIVE

Sharing Sorrow and Strength

Emma's heart beat painfully hard when it became apparent something wasn't right with little Alvin. Her joy of making acquaintance with her firstborn son was immediately smothered by grief. His life was over before it had barely begun.

"No!" she cried, holding her baby close, unwilling to admit that his warmth was already fading. He was cold and unmoving, not unlike the reaction of her spirit.

Emma's shock was only confounded by the physical pain and weakness that entirely consumed her. She was only vaguely aware of Joseph in the room, of her mother telling him the news that Emma still had not fully accepted. When Emma could no longer bear to hold his lifeless form, Joseph took little Alvin, keeping him carefully wrapped in the tiny quilt that Emma had made. His tears expressed her own grief. She wanted to console him, but she felt too shocked to speak, and too sore to move.

The weight of Emma's grief soon passed into illness. Days that had no rhythm of time merged painfully into weeks, while it became difficult to discern between her overwhelming heartache and the malady afflicting her body. Her womb felt as empty as her arms. She concluded that she should have been able to feel the life of her child in one or the other, but his absence in both respects was difficult to grasp. Again she was grateful to have her mother there to help care for her. And Joseph was never far away.

She saw much evidence of his concern for her, and knew he shared her grief over losing their son. But it was difficult to know what to say on either count. She often found him praying at her side, and she was surprised to realize that he feared she would die along with little Alvin. Emma had to consider the possibility herself. Was her time nearly done? Was this the end? At times she felt so terribly ill and wracked with grief that she wanted it to be so. But drifting in and out of delirium, she became reconciled with the knowledge that her time was not yet done on this earth. She had much yet to accomplish, and Joseph needed her.

Emma woke in the dark, not surprised to find Joseph sitting near her bedside. He was bending toward the lamp that burned low on the table, reading from the Bible. Emma studied his countenance while he was unaware, noting the worried crease over his eyes. He rubbed a hand over his face and pressed it to his brow as he planted his elbow on the table. She could see the pain of losing his son etched into his every move. But there was something more; she knew his concerns were more complex than that.

"What is it?" she asked, letting him know she was awake.

Joseph turned and immediately set the Bible aside, moving to the edge of the bed. "How are you?" he asked, pressing a hand over the side of her face and into her hair. She regretted being the cause of the worry she saw in his countenance.

"I'm going to be all right," she whispered. "How are *you?*" He didn't answer, and his smile felt forced. "What is it?" she repeated. "What's wrong?"

"I'm worried for you, Emma," he said. "I need you. I pray every hour that God won't take you away from me as well."

As well. Those two words reminded of her of their loss, and she had to consciously distract herself from the maternal ache she felt. "I'm going to be all right," she repeated and lifted a weak hand to his face. He put his hand over hers to press it there more tightly. "What's wrong?" she asked. "What's troubling you? There's something else." He closed his eyes abruptly as if to avoid the question, but the worry in his expression deepened. "Tell me," she urged.

Joseph lowered his head but drew her hand from his face to hold it tightly in his. "Martin has not returned. Something's wrong. I know it; I can feel it." He lifted his eyes to look at her. "I don't know what to do, Emma."

"Surely there is some logical explanation for his delay."

"Perhaps," he said. "I hope."

Emma immediately knew there was only one thing to be done; she didn't even have to think about it. "You must find out what's wrong, Joseph. You must go."

"But . . ." He shook his head and again closed his eyes. "I don't want to leave you, Emma. I—"

"I'll be fine. You need to go."

"How can I?" he asked with tears brimming in his eyes.

Emma could feel his inner torment and felt consoled by it, but she also knew what was most important. She leaned carefully up onto one elbow to look at him more closely. "Mother will look after me. I'll be fine. You must go, or you'll never find peace."

Emma could see Joseph pondering her words during the ensuing silence. She sensed his dilemma, his reluctance to leave her battling with his fear over what might have happened with Martin. She knew how precious those manuscript pages were and could not imagine the extent of Joseph's concerns. But she meant what she'd said, and repeated it to be sure that he understood. "You must go, Joseph. I'll be fine."

He nodded hesitantly, then eased a little closer and wrapped her in his arms. She clung to him tightly, not wanting him to go, but knowing there was no other option. She would not be whining and complaining and keeping him from the Lord's work.

Saying good-bye was difficult, but she offered him her bravest countenance and assured him that all would be well, saving her tears until he had gone. Again Emma lost her sense of time during Joseph's absence. Each day she felt a little better physically, and she simply tried not to think about the absence of little Alvin. Her mother was compassionate and cared well for Emma. Her father showed concern, but as always, Emma knew that he disapproved of her marriage to Joseph, and he was not happy about the work Joseph was engaged in, which he considered to be utter nonsense. Emma's efforts to convince him otherwise were futile, and she could only attempt to find peace within herself over his belief that Joseph was a fool, and that she was equally foolish for being committed to such a man. All things combined, her grief was difficult to bear, yet she had no choice but to bear it. She could only be grateful that her father was not being outwardly contentious, and she prayed that with time his heart might be softened toward Joseph.

Emma prayed continually that her husband would return safely, and that he would easily resolve whatever might have caused Martin's delay. She thought often of the 116 pages and the many hours of work they had put into the translation. The words contained in those pages were *priceless!* Much of the text had been scribed by her own hand, and the thought of anything happening to it made her sick at heart. She kept telling herself to trust in the Lord and not believe the worst. She wanted to believe that all would be well, and prayed every hour that it would be.

Most days, Emma tried not to dwell on the absence of her baby, but there were times when she simply needed to ponder her deepest feelings, and she wondered how long it might be until they were blessed with another child. On just such a day, Emma carefully refolded all the baby clothes that had been intended for little Alvin. She dreamed of another child, and longed for her emptiness to be filled. The opening of the door startled her, and her heart leapt to realize that Joseph had returned. She turned to see him, then his heavy countenance became readily evident, and fear gripped her as she wondered what had happened. Her joy at seeing him momentarily outweighed her concerns. She had longed for his company every hour of every day. And no one understood the loss of their baby as he did. She needed him!

When their eyes met, nothing mattered but their elation at being together again. He paused and looked at her with eyes that expressed his many emotions. He was relieved to see her up and doing better, but he was still concerned over her health. He was still grieving for the loss of their son, as she was. And something else was wrong; something that frightened her. Unable to consider that for the moment, she took a step forward, and he did the same. As they came into each other's arms, Emma felt his strength fill her. Everything was better simply because he was there. *Everything!* She clung to him tightly, and he to her. He kissed her cheek and buried his face against her throat, murmuring, "Oh, Emma, Emma. My dear, precious Emma." He drew back and took her shoulders into his hands. "You're well?" he asked.

"I'm much better, as you can see," she assured him.

"Oh, how I've prayed for you!" he said.

"That must surely be why I am better." She took his face into her hands and kissed him, grateful beyond words to have him back. But once their greeting was adequately exchanged, the torment in his eyes became more evident. "You must tell me everything."

Joseph nodded, then took hold of her again, embracing her tightly for a long moment. With no words spoken, she knew that he needed her as much as she needed him, and that their loneliness while apart from each other had been mutual.

"Tell me what's happened," Emma said, and he sank onto a chair. His despair was starkly evident, and Emma's heart tightened with fear. She wondered what could be so dire.

"The manuscript is lost," he said, and Emma gasped. She couldn't believe it. With all she'd imagined that might have gone wrong, it had never occurred to her that something like this could happen. She put a hand over the tightening in her chest and attempted to draw a full breath.

"Martin promised he wouldn't let anything happen to it," she insisted, as if saying so might make it true.

Joseph planted his elbows on the table, pressing his head into his hands. She'd never seen him so upset. "I should have done what the Lord told me to do the first time," he muttered, and she realized he was crying. "It was wrong of me . . . to keep asking." His tone was almost angry, but she knew it was not toward her. She was amazed to realize he was not angry with Martin, either. It was himself that he blamed. "I should have listened; should have trusted Him. I feared man more than God, Emma."

Recalling conversations prior to Martin's taking the manuscript, she couldn't believe it had come to this. "I never imagined that such a thing would happen."

"Nor did I." Joseph wiped his face with his shirtsleeve. "But the record is lost, Emma, and I am responsible." Despair consumed his countenance. "I fear that my soul is lost, as well."

Emma didn't know what to say. How could she possibly console him? That night she prayed with him and for him, but she felt helpless to assuage his grief and concerns. The loss of their child quickly became swallowed up in this unanticipated tragedy. Emma knew that Joseph shared her grief, but she also knew that the Lord's work had to take precedence over all else. So she cried her tears in private and prayed for the strength to give her husband the support he needed. Still, he seemed beyond consoling. Her helplessness on his behalf only deepened when he told her he had been severely chastised by the angel Moroni, and the plates had been taken back. She couldn't even imagine how such an encounter might have transpired, nor how difficult it must have been for Joseph. He took to working ridiculously hard, as if he could somehow drive away his anguish by keeping busy every waking moment. Emma felt certain that her husband felt lost with this detachment from the work that he knew in his heart he'd been called to do. Her heart ached for him, and she struggled to find words that would give him comfort and hope. Holding a prayer in her heart, as always, she was waiting for him when he came in from a long day's work. Even at a glance, she sensed once again that his intense attention to such hard work was merely an attempt to distract himself from all that weighed on him.

Emma could almost visibly see his burden as she approached him, putting a hand to his face, finding it streaked with dirt and sweat. He said nothing, and barely met her eyes, as if he were ashamed to face her.

Emma silently prayed, *Please, Father. Guide my words. Help me give him the strength to go on.* Not feeling any great inspiration, she finally asked, "How are you?"

"I've jeopardized everything, Emma," he said.

"And what more can you do to make it right, Joseph? You've done everything that you can possibly—"

"I'm not certain that I could ever do enough to make up for this," he countered. Emma took a step back, overcome with sorrow on his behalf as she considered the aura of self-punishment surrounding him.

The silence became strained, and again she prayed. Words came to her mind, simple but firm. With tenderness she repeated them. "I believe that God is merciful and forgiving, Joseph. Surely you are entitled to that forgiveness and mercy."

Joseph lifted his head abruptly. Emma held her breath, praying that her words would soften his heart, that he would remember the cumulative evidence he had been given of the Lord's boundless mercy and love. He turned to meet her eyes, and Emma saw there the first glimmer of hope that she'd seen since his discovery of the loss of the manuscript. He stood to face her, and the hope she saw eased into understanding, and a sparkle of peace. She smiled, and he took her into his arms, as if holding her close might help reinforce the hope she longed to give him. In that moment she was struck with the power of their marriage commitment, that they were bound together in sustaining each other through the challenges of life—whatever they might be. He had carried her through many sorrows. She only hoped that she could always do the same for him.

In time the plates were given back to Joseph, with the instruction that he was not to retranslate what had been lost. A new understanding was opened as it became evident that the Lord had apparently known long ago that this would happen, and records had been kept centuries earlier that compensated for the loss. It did not eliminate Joseph's accountability in the choices he'd made, but there was comfort in knowing that the Lord's plan would not be frustrated. They were relieved to know that Joseph's calling had not been jeopardized, and that the power of repentance was real. Joseph told Emma more than once that he would never quibble with the Lord again. From this experience, he learned to do as he was instructed; nothing less and no deviation to any degree would be acceptable. He never again wanted to suffer such regret or come under such condemnation. He felt certain no earthly misery could be heavier than that.

As with all that Joseph endured, Emma learned the same lessons at his side. She could not foresee what the Lord might require of them, but she shared Joseph's conviction to do whatever the Lord asked. And she prayed that whatever that might be, she would be equal to it and not falter.

For a time the plates remained untouched beneath the bed. Even though they were in his possession, Joseph was not permitted to translate. And Emma never looked at them. Joseph had told her not to. Those weeks were filled with peace except for the ongoing ache Emma felt as she longed for a child to fill her empty arms. She and Joseph talked often of their grief, and she continually marveled at how his love sustained her so fully. They were united in all things; that knowledge and the evidence of it could surely carry her through any hardship.

Joseph shifted his focus to working the land that he had purchased from Emma's father. She imagined it one day thriving with whatever might be planted there, and anticipated raising their family here in this place that had always been home to her. She also clung to the hope that eventually her father's heart would be fully softened toward Joseph, and she could enjoy the love of her husband *and* the acceptance of her father. Ironically, Isaac Hale was pleased to see Joseph working the land. It seemed that Joseph could only find favor with her father when he was being denied the opportunity and permission to do the work God had commissioned him to do. As long as her father couldn't accept that Joseph truly was acting as God's servant, Emma knew they would always be at cross-purposes.

Emma once again had the privilege of being a scribe for Joseph as the translation resumed. She occasionally thought of all of her carefully written words that had been lost, but she reminded herself that the past could not be changed, and they needed to focus only on the work to be done from that time forward.

While Joseph sat at the table across from her, keeping the plates from her view, he spoke the words of the prophet Nephi with fluent clarity. "'I caused that they should hide themselves without the walls . . .'"

He paused and asked, "Emma, did Jerusalem have a wall around it?"

Emma was struck with one more piece of evidence that this work was divine and not of Joseph's own invention. She simply smiled and said, "Yes . . . it did."

Joseph made a contemplative noise and continued. A few minutes later he said, "The next word is spelled S-A-R-I-A-H."

Emma carefully wrote the unique name, pondered briefly how it looked on paper, and continued writing as he spoke. Hour after hour he dictated without hesitation or deviation. She knew Joseph well enough to know that he could barely write a well-worded letter, let alone a book. This very fact manifested to Emma the marvel of what was taking place. Being his wife, she was also keenly aware of how he was learning from the words he translated, and at times she could almost visibly see the subtle but ever-present development of his character as the Lord molded him for whatever might lie ahead. They were learning and growing together. At times when they were not working on the translation, they often talked of the principles unfolding before them. Emma loved to hear Joseph analyze them deeply; he had a great desire to discuss the light being shed on facets of religion that had always left him uneasy or perplexed. Occasionally she came up with an insight that took their discussions to a deeper level, and she would wonder how she might have ever survived being married to a man who did not share her desire to think deeply and continually stretch and grow through the consideration of new ideas.

Every hour that Emma spent as scribe while Joseph translated left her more in awe of the greatness of the work her husband was called to do. Still, it was evident, as it had been before, that she could not maintain their household and be able to help him as much as he needed. It was therefore a tremendous blessing when a young man named Oliver Cowdery came to their home. He had been staying with Joseph's family in Palmyra, and there he had heard much of Joseph's experiences and endeavors. He had come to offer his help with such great conviction and sincerity that it was evident he had most assuredly been guided there by the hand of the Lord.

Emma observed an immediate bond between Joseph and Oliver and was grateful for the support that this man offered. As they worked together, the translation moved forward smoothly.

Joseph made no effort to engage in farming or any other type of labor, knowing that he needed to dedicate himself wholly to the work, trusting that the Lord would provide for their needs—much to her father's chagrin. At times it became difficult, and there was cause for concern, but miracles did indeed occur, and all was well. In fact, many great and marvelous things happened during the course of Oliver's stay. Emma was continually amazed at the reports of progress she received from her husband. She was especially thrilled to learn that the power of the holy priesthood, which had not been present upon the earth for many centuries, had been restored by divine means. It was nearly impossible to comprehend such grand events and the gentle simplicity with which they occurred. Although she was no longer involved in dictation, she was always anxious to learn as Joseph recounted to her the events of the translation and the ongoing revelations that were being manifested to him and Oliver.

Emma's favorite time of day was late at night when she and Joseph would lay with their heads close together on the same pillow and talk of the wonders that were taking place. She loved to hear him repeat the miracles he'd witnessed, and the marvels of the Lord's blessings. Some stories he told over and over, and she never grew tired of hearing them. Each line and precept strengthened her knowledge that his mission was holy and his purpose divine. And she felt continually grateful to be the woman by his side, the handmaid of the Lord privileged enough to be privy to such wonders. She felt humbled, and was often overcome with emotions too complex to express. She only prayed that she would not let the Lord—or her husband—down. Her father was an entirely different matter. Emma longed to share with both of her parents the glorious events taking place around her, and to have them share in the thrill of all she had felt. But her mother would not become involved in anything that went against her husband's approval, and Emma's every attempt to talk to her father with the hope of renewing the closeness they'd once shared always left her disappointed.

"Joseph has been called by God to do this work, Father," she told him, not for the first time. Somehow, their conversations always managed to come around to the same thing. "I am his wife; I must support him in what he's doing."

"Work?" Isaac bellowed. "What *work?* I don't see him doing anything to provide a living for you, or—"

"He's doing the Lord's work," Emma protested, putting great effort into remaining calm. "The Lord will provide."

Isaac shook his head in disgust. "Your husband is a fool and a dreamer, Emma, and he's making a fool out of you. You haven't even *seen* this 'gold Bible.' You can't possibly know if it's even real." Emma couldn't answer. He'd struck a nerve, and she wondered if he knew it. She *hadn't* seen the plates. As much as she'd wanted to, she'd never taken so much as a peek. That very morning while she'd been working in the kitchen, they had been there on the table, covered with a towel. No one had been around, no one would have noticed if she'd lifted the covering—just a little. She'd pressed her fingers over them, had felt the texture beneath the fabric. She'd fondled the edges, marveling at the distinct separation of each page of gold. But she had resisted the urge to look, knowing that *God* would know. And Joseph had asked her not to. She was determined to honor her husband *and* God. After all, she knew for a fact that Joseph and God shared a close relationship. She could not betray the trust of one without offending the other.

Now, hearing her father's demeaning words, Emma almost wished she *had* looked, if only so she could tell him that she *wasn't* a fool, and neither was Joseph. But such thoughts were quickly assuaged by the knowledge that she'd done the right thing. And there *was* one thing she could tell her father with conviction. "I just know."

Isaac Hale made a noise of disgust and stormed out of the room. Emma remained where she was and cried, wishing her father's approval was not so important to her—and so out of reach. She overcame her moment of self-pity with the firm reminder that she absolutely *knew* the Book of Mormon was of divine authenticity. She didn't have the slightest doubt of it. And she knew that such conviction would carry her through.

Emma tried not to hold onto the hurt of her father's words, but they often jumped into her mind and stung her heart. The need for them to go to New York for a time relieved the tension between the men Emma loved, but she knew such relief was only temporary.

Once again the Lord proved that He would meet their needs as the Whitmer family in Fayette opened their home to Joseph and Oliver, and Emma as well. The Whitmers' home was located not so many miles from Joseph's family, and it was wonderful to see them all again. The kindness and generosity of the Whitmer family was added evidence of the Lord's tender mercies, and Emma quickly grew fond of Mary Whitmer, who was gracious and kind in sharing her home. David Whitmer and Oliver both assisted Joseph in the ongoing translation of the plates, while Emma did her best to remain supportive and not wonder when they could go back to Harmony. As much as she missed her family, her thoughts were more often drawn to the little grave where her baby was buried. She longed for a child to ease the ache of her empty arms, but mostly kept such thoughts to herself, not wanting to burden Joseph with them when the work that consumed him was so important. Still, there were moments when her grief refused to be held back, usually late at night when they were completely alone and there was no one or nothing to interrupt the quiet around them. She would share her deepest thoughts and cry in his arms, always finding strength from the evidence that he shared her grief and understood her concerns for the future. And with the common bonds they shared, she always found the courage to go on.

Emma wiped another stray tear and attempted to focus on the task at hand, wanting to keep busy enough to not think about the less-than-favorable words exchanged between her and Joseph only minutes before he'd gone upstairs to join Oliver and David and work on the translation. Emma hadn't intended to cause any annoyance or difficulty for Joseph; she'd simply let her own frustrations get out of hand. At moments such as this, her thoughts and feelings vacillated between her own human needs and frailty, and the undeniably unique circumstances surrounding her marriage. There were times when she could see Joseph only as a man, mildly inconsiderate and predictably fallible. She'd never expected him to be perfect, even though she knew that some people did. But perhaps at times her expectations were still too high. He certainly had the right to be human. In spite of his being a prophet, the same principle surely applied to all men—and women—in all walks of life. It certainly applied to *her.* She couldn't help thinking that perhaps her own inadequacies were far too many to make her capable of standing by such a man through the challenges of a life that could never be normal. He *was* a prophet of God, and sometimes that very fact was difficult to understand or even remember amidst everyday living. She, more than anyone, saw his ongoing struggle to understand his place in this work and what exactly the Lord expected of him. She admired and honored him, as she knew he did her. Still, the memory of his recent words stung. He'd not been cruel or harsh; she doubted it was in him to be so. But she wondered if he had any idea how his insensitivity had wounded her. The situation was worsened by her near-certainty that Oliver and David—as well as other members of the Whitmer family—had to be aware of what had transpired.

Emma wiped another tear, then focused more fully on cleaning the dishes, convinced that she should stop feeling sorry for herself over such a trivial matter. She was startled to hear footsteps on the stairs. Then the door opened and closed. A quick glimpse through the window let her know it was Joseph. She wondered where he might be going, and hoped that something wasn't wrong. About an hour later he returned. She pretended to be distracted by a window that needed cleaning, seeming oblivious to his entering the house. She expected him to hurry by and continue his work, knowing that Oliver and David were likely waiting. When she didn't hear his boots on the stairs, she turned and found him standing behind her, his eyes tender, his countenance humble. She marveled at how just seeing him look at her that way could erase every tiny measure of frustration or care.

"Emma," he muttered and reached out a hand toward her. "Forgive me."

Emma took in his words and felt them soothe her, heart and soul. She stepped forward to take his outstretched hand, then she eased into his arms, fully embracing his apology.

Joseph urged her to sit close beside him while he told her what he'd learned in the past hour about the powers of heaven being inseparably connected to humility and faith. Emma treasured the moment in the midst of their busy lives, almost grateful now for the incident between them that had prompted such a sweet experience. Joseph spoke to her with all the sensitivity of a tender husband, and with the strength and courage of a prophet who clearly understood the need to have everything in its proper order. After he returned to his work, Emma returned to hers with a light heart, humming a happy song.

That night as Joseph climbed into bed beside her, he spoke softly of his love for her. He echoed her own thoughts as he admitted to his ongoing grief over the loss of their little Alvin. They cried together, then spoke of their hope for another child. She asked him how the translation was coming along, then she lit a candle and leaned on one elbow while he spoke, wanting to see his face as he shared both the wondrous stories coming forth from the ancient record and the glimpses he'd been given of the great restoration of the gospel that was beginning to unfold. At such moments Emma felt no grief or heartache—only hope and perfect peace. She was truly blessed among women to have claimed the heart of such a man, and to have found favor enough in God's eyes to assist in such a marvelous work.

Not many days following, Joseph told Emma that the translation was nearly finished. He told her that God had revealed to him that a few would be privileged to see the plates for themselves, so that they could be witnesses to their actual existence. Emma couldn't help hoping that she might be among them. Conversations with her father over that very matter strengthened her hope that she might be privileged enough to see the plates. She was bruised more deeply than she wanted to admit when Joseph told her who had been chosen—and she was not among them. Martin Harris *was* chosen—even though he had caused so much grief for Joseph when the manuscript pages had been lost. Emma understood the power of repentance, and she was grateful to know that Martin had returned to good standing with the Lord. But was she somehow less worthy?

Emma struggled internally over the matter, vacillating between an indulgence in self-pity and then scolding herself for feeling so petty. What bothered her most of all was knowing that Mary Whitmer had seen the plates. She'd told Emma herself. Mary had done much for them; she'd opened her home and had labored unceasingly to keep everything in order and everyone fed while the work continued. And Mary had also made personal sacrifices. But hadn't Emma proven herself as well? She didn't understand why she felt the way she did, but when it became evident she couldn't talk herself out of her feelings, she told Joseph exactly how she *did* feel.

"I don't understand," she said while her husband dried the dishes she had just washed.

"It was not up to me, Emma," Joseph said.

"I realize that, but . . . Mary saw the plates." She pushed a dirty plate into the sudsy water, then put her wet hands on her hips, facing her husband squarely. "Am I not faithful enough?" Her voice cracked. "Have I not done as you asked?"

"Emma." Joseph protested the very idea simply by the tone of his voice. "Sometimes our faith is tested, but surely the Lord knows, as I do, that this is not a reflection of your worthiness."

Emma found it difficult to believe him, and left him to finish the dishes on his own. Perhaps she just needed time to let her own emotions settle. If not for her father's disdain over the matter, perhaps she wouldn't have felt so hurt and confused.

Gradually Emma felt her anger melt into the sorrow beneath it. She prayed to understand and find peace over the matter. She didn't want to feel so self-absorbed and upset. With time she felt the answers come; however, they didn't come quickly or easily, but rather with much wrestling. Yet peace *did* come to replace her heartache. Her personal bond with her Father in Heaven became strengthened by the evidence of His great care. Through the Spirit she came to see that it wasn't selfish to want her father's approval, but it *was* important to remember that it was not the approval of *any* man—not even her husband—that could supersede the need to do God's will. Emma knew that God was with her in her struggles, and that He always would be so long as she strove to remain faithful. While she still wondered about her place in all that was happening, she came to know that her exclusion from viewing the plates was not any indication of her own faithfulness—or the lack of it. She also knew that God's plans were beyond her understanding, and perhaps most importantly, Emma came to know that Mary's privilege of seeing the plates was no reflection of Emma's own personal worthiness. This had been a tender mercy extended to Mary, something that was between Mary and the Lord and something that Emma could likely never fully understand. Emma learned then that it was impossible to compare herself, her thoughts, her feelings, her experiences, or her blessings with those of any other woman—because only God could fully know a woman's heart. And God knew hers.

The translation of the plates was completed, and the sacred record was returned to the care of the Angel Moroni—and Emma never saw them. While occasionally she felt a little tug at her heart in that regard, deep inside she was all right with that. She didn't *have* to see them to know that they were real. It was as she'd told her father—there are some things you know with your heart, that you might never know with your head—or see with your eyes.

CHAPTER SIX

Elect Lady

By the end of March, the Book of Mormon was finished. Joseph's joy at holding the printed book in his hands filled Emma's heart. She shared his joy completely as she held it herself and touched the words on the pages, pondering the depth of their meaning and all that she knew Joseph had endured to see this day come to pass. She knew more than *anyone* how difficult the work had been, and for that reason she perhaps best understood the fulfillment he surely felt to see it published and ready to share with anyone who might read it with an open heart.

"We did it, Emma," Joseph said and embraced her. They laughed together, then sat down to look the book over more carefully. Emma couldn't wait to read it!

At the first possible moment, that very day, Emma began to read the Book of Mormon, and she took every possible opportunity that she could to continue reading. The closeness of the Spirit often warmed her heart as she pondered many of the book's passages. Some of what she read was familiar because she had heard the words come forth as she wrote them down; other parts were familiar because Joseph had told her about them.

One night she couldn't sleep and found herself drawn to reading instead. Though her eyes hurt and her head felt heavy, her desire to read was more powerful. Candles were dear and precious, but her compelling need to read was stronger, and she quietly slipped out of bed. Engrossed in her reading, she was startled to note that her heart had quickened dramatically, and she went back to reread and discover what might have caused such a reaction.

And thus prophesied Joseph saying: . . . From the previous text, Emma knew that meant Joseph of Egypt . . . *Behold, that seer will the Lord bless; and they that seek to destroy him shall be confounded; for this promise, which I have obtained of the Lord, of the fruit of my loins, shall be fulfilled. Behold, I am sure of the fulfilling of this promise; And his name shall be called after me; and it shall be after the name of his father.*

Emma gasped. Did that mean what it seemed to mean? *Yes,* a voice inside of her seemed to say. She struggled to take in a deep breath and pressed a hand over her quickened heart. How could it be possible? But it *was!* The truth of it was undeniable as it filled her entire being. The ancient prophet Joseph was foretelling her husband's work—and he was being very specific. She read that last line again. *And his name shall be called after me; and it shall be after the name of his father.*

"Praise be to God," she murmured under her breath and read on. *And he shall be like unto me; for the thing, which the Lord shall bring forth by his hand, by the power of the Lord shall bring my people unto salvation.*

"Did you say something?" Joseph asked and startled her.

"Oh!" she said while her heart pounded for an entirely different reason. "You scared me!"

"Sorry," he said and moved her hair from over her shoulder to kiss the side of her neck. "It's the middle of the night, Emma. You should sleep."

"I can't," she insisted, then teased, "It's a very compelling book. You should read it."

He chuckled and put his hands on her shoulders. "I am rather familiar with it."

"Then perhaps you could explain this to me," she said, pointing at the phrases she'd just read.

Joseph leaned forward to read silently, and she watched his expression closely. She saw understanding in his eyes, but he said with easy nonchalance, "It means that . . . the Lord will raise up a seer to—"

"I understand what it means," she said. "Does this mean you?"

"I have not yet begun to understand the Lord's purposes for me, Emma," he said with perfect humility. She knew he was well aware of what it meant, but wondered if he'd ever admit it.

"A seer named Joseph . . . after the name of his father."

He sat down and she saw his eyes become distant, then they focused fully on her, and she saw the vulnerability there. His voice broke with a whisper, as if he didn't want the walls to overhear. "How can it be me, Emma? Look at me. I'm just . . . a simple farm boy. I can barely read and write."

"Which makes this work all the more a miracle, Joseph." She wrapped his hand in both of hers. "If God had wanted a university professor to do this work, he would have chosen one. But he chose *you.*"

"I know, Emma," he said, and a single tear trickled down his face. She wiped it away, and he went on. "I know He chose me. There is no room for me to question it. But there are times when . . . I wonder how it's possible; times when I . . . cannot comprehend the truth of what I know. How can I be this great seer, Emma?" More tears came, and he quickly brushed them away. "When I think of that day . . . sometimes I wonder . . . what I might have felt if I'd had any inclination of what would happen. I was only a boy, Emma, a boy with a simple question—or at least it seemed simple to me at the time. And look at what has happened." He reached out a hand to reverently touch the Book of Mormon, laying open on the table. "How can it be me, Emma?"

"Oh, Joseph," she said, gently pushing his hair back off his face, "God knows you by name. He spoke to you. I'm certain all that He expects of you is what you've given all along—the best that you have. He will make up the difference."

"But . . . I've made so many mistakes, Emma. When I didn't listen to Him and gave Martin the—"

"Hush." She put her fingers over his lips. "You *are* human, Joseph. No one—especially not God—would expect you to be anything more. We all make mistakes. God has forgiven you, and you need to forgive yourself. You must never lose sight of the fact that God *has* chosen you. With that knowledge in your heart—and I know that it is there—you must trust in Him to guide your steps. And He *will* make up the difference, Joseph. I know that He will."

Emma saw him smile, and the vulnerability in his eyes was replaced by the self-assurance that was more like him. It was not in his character to be anything less than humble and to readily recognize the source of his strength. But in his countenance shone the simple knowledge that he was indeed a man who had spoken with God—face-to-face. He unquestionably knew his mission was great, but the uncertainty of what exactly might be required was surely unnerving. At times it felt unnerving for *her,* but as close as she was to Joseph, she was not the direct vessel of God's work. She could only do her best to take her own advice and remember that God had chosen her as well, if only to stand by Joseph's side. She had to simply do her best to encourage and support him, with the faith that God would make up the difference for her as well.

"You will surely be great in God's eyes, Joseph—when all is said and done."

"And how do you know that, Emma?" he asked, smiling again. "Has the Lord shown you my future?"

"Don't be silly." She laughed softly, then became more serious. "He doesn't have to, Joseph. I know your heart. I know that nothing is more important to you than doing God's will. With such desires in your heart, how could He not be pleased with all that you do on His behalf?"

He lifted her hand to his lips and pressed a lingering kiss there before he said, "You keep reminding me of that, Emma. As long as you are by my side, how can I go wrong?"

Emma glanced down, briefly unsettled by the thought. "Don't rely on me too heavily," she said. "I'm merely human, Joseph, and sometimes slow to accept God's will."

"And once you do, you never waver," he said, again kissing her hand. "You are precious to me, Emma, as you are to the Lord." He stood up and urged her to do the same. "Now, come to bed. It's very, very late and we both need some sleep. You can read tomorrow." Emma glanced at the book with yearning but knew he was right.

The following morning, as soon as she'd done the bare minimum of her responsibilities about the house, Emma returned to her reading and kept at it every possible minute. A few days later when she was nearing the end, she walked into the yard with the book, in order to be alone. As she read, she was struck by the challenge written by Moroni near the end of his record—that same Moroni who had instructed Joseph as a heavenly messenger. *And when ye shall receive these things, I would exhort you that ye would ask God, the Eternal Father, in the name of Christ, if these things are not true; and if ye shall ask with a sincere heart, with real intent, having faith in Christ, he will manifest the truth of it unto you, by the power of the Holy Ghost; And by the power of the Holy Ghost ye may know the truth of all things.*

Emma took the message into her heart and realized with a surety that she had known the truth all along. From the very first time she had heard words from the record coming from Joseph's mouth, something deep inside had recognized its truthfulness, and the Holy Ghost *had* reaffirmed that witness, again and again.

Bursting with excitement, Emma returned to the house and immediately went to find Joseph. "Oh, Joseph," she said, and he looked pleasantly amused by her enthusiasm. "It's true! It's all true." She laughed and set the book aside to take both his hands into hers. "I mean . . . I knew all along that it was . . . but now I know even more . . . deeply."

Tears came to accentuate her joy, and through them she saw tears gather in Joseph's eyes as well. "Yes," he said and wrapped her in his arms, "it *is* true, Emma." He took hold of her shoulders and added with a trembling voice, "Millions will find joy through this book, Emma, as they are led to the truthfulness of the gospel. But there is no one—*no one*—whose knowledge of its truthfulness means more to me than yours."

Emma nodded and swallowed a fresh rise of emotion as her joy blossomed even further. When she found the voice to speak, she said, "I'm very glad you feel that way, because . . . I certainly do." She laughed softly and wiped her tears. "And perhaps this will be the answer to your mother's prayers . . . that your parents will finally be united in their faith."

Joseph's smile broadened, and again his eyes were moist as he said, "Miracles certainly have not ceased."

"No, they certainly have not," she said and silently thanked her Father in Heaven for blessing her life so richly. With the truth of the gospel being restored to the earth, and the love of her good husband to give her such happiness, she had to believe in her heart that the miracles were only beginning.

With the Book of Mormon now printed, it quickly became evident that the work would roll forth. On the sixth day of April, a new church was organized by Joseph under the Lord's direction—although he made it clear that it was not *new,* but rather a restoration of the pure gospel of Jesus Christ as it had once been.

Emma knew the truth of that principle in her heart, and she felt unbridled joy to be present on such a great day. The pride she felt in her husband and his accomplishments was overshadowed by the warmth in her heart, reaffirming to her once again that he was a prophet of God.

As the book circulated, along with the testimonies of those who had come to know for themselves of its truthfulness, many people began gathering in the area. Baptisms were performed, and the Church grew quickly. Emma shared Joseph's joy at witnessing the happiness of others as they became a part of the fold. And she felt a more personal fulfillment in seeing her husband's growing confidence in his mission. At times he privately shared his concerns over his own feelings of inadequacy. She would then remind him of all that he'd accomplished thus far, and of the mighty miracles he'd been privy to, and he would press forward. Each day she saw him settle a little more comfortably into his role—not only as the man chosen to bring forth this work through his personal connection to God, but as the public figure these people were looking to for guidance and strength. His kindness and quiet generosity were as profound as his ability to deliver a stirring sermon with no premeditation—only divine inspiration.

A truly great moment for Joseph was seeing his father baptized into the only true church on the earth. Emma observed their embrace after Father Smith stepped out of the water, then she exchanged a warm glance with Lucy, knowing their thoughts were the same. Lucy had told Emma she'd been praying for many years that she and her husband could be united in their faith. And now they were. It was truly a miracle! Emma also recalled that Lucy had given her hope that her own prayers would be answered, that her father's heart would one day be softened. She continued to pray for it every day, longing for the time when she might once again have favor in her father's eyes.

In direct proportion to the quiet miracles, persecution and difficulty mounted. It seemed that Joseph could do nothing without drawing the attention of evildoers who were intent on disrupting the work, and even causing Joseph harm. Emma struggled at times to hold to her faith and trust that God would preserve her husband and keep him safe. It became so bad that on the day when Emma was baptized, along with several others, their gathering was interrupted by a mob. To have this sacred event in her life marred by such madness was difficult for her to contend with. But, as always, Joseph reminded her to let go of anger and remember that all souls were precious in the eyes of God.

Emma's fears mounted when another meeting was interrupted and Joseph was arrested on false charges. *Arrested!* Emma was horrified that something such as this could happen in a country that was *supposed* to be grounded in religious freedom. She wondered why people couldn't just leave well enough alone and allow them to worship in peace. She was frantic wondering what might be happening to Joseph and what the outcome of his trial might be. It took the effort of many friends and associates to defend him, but he was no sooner acquitted than he was arrested again and once more required to face many false testimonies laid out against him. Being separated from him was difficult enough without having to entertain unthinkable thoughts. She couldn't even imagine what might happen if he was declared guilty of ridiculous accusations that had no basis in truth whatsoever. Her countless prayers were answered when again he was cleared of all charges. Emma was so happy to see him alive and well that she never wanted to let him out of her sight again. A nagging inner voice lured her to believe that this was only the beginning of such atrocities, but she ignored such thoughts and chose instead to enjoy every minute with her husband.

Due to ongoing difficulties, Joseph was often driven to extreme measures to protect himself. Joseph and other leaders of the Church were forced at times to keep themselves in seclusion to avoid trouble, and Emma could only pray that they would all remain safe. Her faith was strengthened by Joseph's determination to not allow any opposition to hold back the growth of the Church. But she continually wrestled with worrying over her husband's well-being. She felt safer once they had gone back to their home in Pennsylvania, even though there were troubles there as well. Emma enjoyed being near her family again, and simply tried to ignore the way that her father kept a cold distance from Joseph, regularly making his feelings known to Emma over the matter. Wondering if there would ever be peace with her father again, she chose to focus on the love she'd found in her marriage, and to be supportive of her husband's endeavors.

With the need for the gospel to go out into the world, Joseph called many to serve missions—to leave home and family and set out to preach the word, often with little or nothing to go on but faith that the Lord would provide for their needs. Emma took the opportunity to make a coat for Parley Pratt, a dear man who had become a fast friend to Joseph through his conviction of their shared beliefs. Parley would be walking a thousand miles, preaching all the way, and he was in sore need of a coat. To Emma, it seemed like a small contribution to the cause, but Parley was grateful—and so was Joseph.

With so much taking place in regard to the Church, Emma was intrigued one morning to hear Joseph say, "Emma, I received a very special revelation."

Emma's interest was piqued as she wondered what glorious doctrine or principle might have been given to him this time. She was keenly aware of the ongoing revelations he received, and loved to hear him talk about them.

"Tell me," she said and sat down, taking note of the paper in his hand. She considered, not for the first time, how this man she loved was, on occasion, taking dictation from God. She wondered what marvelous words might be on the page he held.

"It's for you, Emma," he said and handed it to her as he sat close by.

"Me?" she questioned, a little breathless. She glanced quickly over the words and saw her name. Joseph eased a little closer and took her hand, holding it tightly while she read through the revelation carefully. She marveled that such words could be for her, and about her; that such a thing could come directly from the Lord on her behalf. But at the same time, she knew it was true; it was real. She knew it in her heart, and she did not doubt it. When she was finished reading she looked into her husband's eyes and felt the truth of it all over again.

"Help me understand," she said softly, looking again at the words on the page.

They talked for a long while of the things the Lord was asking Emma to do, and Joseph shared deeper insights on his feelings over the matter. Still, Emma felt as if she had only begun to understand the implications. That evening as they were finishing supper, Emma asked her husband more specifically what he believed the Lord had meant by referring to her in the revelation as an "elect lady." He spoke to her with typical tenderness of her great value in the eyes of the Lord, of her potential, and of all that she would accomplish through the special gifts God had given her.

Emma wanted to believe such a notion, but she couldn't deny the doubts that filled her mind, conversations with her father mingled among them. When she verbalized her thoughts, Emma was surprised by Joseph's startled expression. The way he looked at her conveyed more than words ever could. He might as well have said, *How could you ever wonder about such a thing?* He reached across the table to take her hand, reminding her of all she had done to help and support him, and his gentle assurance of his great reliance on her comforted her in a way that felt deeply personal and profound. In that moment, with Joseph's hand in hers, and the conviction in his eyes, she *felt* like an elect lady, and an inner warmth soothed her doubts away. How could she question the word of the Lord *and* his prophet—who just happened to be her husband?

With that settled more firmly in her mind, she decided that now would be a good time to tell Joseph something he needed to know. "We're going to have a baby, Mr. Smith," she said with no forewarning.

His joyful response didn't disappoint her. He laughed and hugged her, sharing her joy in the prospect of having a baby.

Together they washed the dishes and put the kitchen in order. Emma thought back to when she'd first looked into his eyes. At the time, she couldn't have imagined loving him more. But she loved him more every day of their lives that they shared. She wished that her father could see how thoroughly happy she was.

As Emma's second pregnancy progressed, she felt new hope blossom inside of her. The death of little Alvin still tugged at her heart, and she longed for her arms to be filled with a child of her own to love and nurture. When her thoughts kept bringing her to an idea over and over, she finally shared it with her husband. She just couldn't ignore the feeling that she might be carrying twins. As they talked of the added joy that might come with *two* babies, Emma felt sure that their loss of little Alvin would be made up.

Along with the sweet anticipation of finally becoming a mother, Emma pondered daily the Lord's message to her in the revelation given through Joseph. More and more she felt its power and importance in her life, and the undeniable knowledge that these words truly had come from God. They were full of deep truth, of things that only God could know. Emma found great comfort and strength in what she'd been told, and she prayed to understand it more fully and to live up to all that the Lord expected of her. She was especially drawn to the concept that a song of the heart was a prayer unto God. Emma had always loved music, and she loved to sing. Had God given her that love to prepare her to compile the hymns for the Church? Did He know the praise and honor she felt for Him when she sang such hymns? Somehow she knew that He did. And somehow He knew that she would need the guidance and strength she had gained from such knowledge. But she never would have imagined how much.

Persecution surrounding Joseph's work worsened, and the only possible option was clear. But when it became evident that there was no choice but to leave Harmony in order to solve the problems, Emma's sadness was difficult to contain, although she couldn't argue the point that it was likely best to have some distance between Joseph and her father. For all of Joseph's efforts to be polite and respectful to Isaac Hale, nothing had changed. Emma was saddened to leave her father. In spite of all the discord between them, she'd never let go of the hope that he might come around. She'd believed that grandchildren might soften him, but she feared that if they moved away now, her parents would never know the children she and Joseph might have one day. And this time she knew they would never be coming back; somehow she just knew. She could hardly admit, even to herself, that leaving here didn't just mean leaving behind another home; it meant abandoning all the dreams she'd indulged in regarding the pleasant future she and Joseph might share in this place. But Emma couldn't think about that. It all had to be left behind, and she could only look to the future.

While packing to leave, Emma pondered the closeness she'd once shared with her father. They'd had a special bond throughout much of her life, an irony that tore at her under the present circumstances. She wished and prayed that he could only look past his prejudice and apprehensions and get a glimpse of the incredible man that Joseph was. But it was not to be. Leaving her father behind—and the hopes that she'd had on his behalf—would be difficult, but Emma wondered how she would ever manage without her mother. Elizabeth Hale had quietly encouraged Emma to be patient with her father, certain that eventually he *would* come around. But now Emma wondered if it would ever happen.

Emma appreciated her mother's help with the packing, and she savored their time together, fearing it would be a very long time—if ever—before she saw her mother again.

CHAPTER SEVEN

The Hand of Hatred

Returning to New York was good in many respects, but it soon became evident they were to move once again. Because of successful missionary work at Kirtland, Ohio, Joseph had a visit from two men named Sidney Rigdon and Edward Partridge, who enthusiastically shared with Joseph the great growth of the Church in that area. These men invited them to move to Kirtland. After much prayer, Joseph received a revelation confirming that it was God's will to remove the Church to Ohio. Joseph Knight took Joseph and Emma there in his sleigh. Emma struggled with the uncertainty, but she knew they were in God's hands and were doing their best to go where He led them. She had to believe there was purpose for their moving on, even if she didn't understand it.

As they set out, Emma said for the sake of conversation, "I understand that we need to go to Ohio, but why in the middle of winter?"

"An adventure!" Joseph said and laughed. Putting an arm around her shoulders he added, "I've made this my rule, Emma: when the Lord commands, do it."

Emma already knew his rule—very well, in fact. But it was still nice to hear that he hadn't wavered in his convictions.

The drive to Kirtland was long and cold. Emma fought to keep her spirits up and not complain, but she wondered if Joseph had any idea where they would even stay once they arrived. Her concern turned to astonishment when they went directly to the store of a Mr. Whitney. It was one of those moments when she could not deny the divine calling possessed by her husband. He called Mr. Whitney by name—a man he had never met—then introduced himself as a prophet. Mr. Whitney was so pleased that he immediately offered them accommodations. Once again, Emma could not deny that the Lord had provided for their needs.

Soon Joseph and Emma were settled in a small house that was built for them on the Morley settlement, near town. The Morleys were good people and Emma quickly grew to care for them and appreciate their conviction in the gospel, which naturally made them eager to help Joseph and his loved ones. It seemed they were continually at the mercy of such people, but Emma recognized that was the Lord's way of providing for their needs and at the same time giving others the opportunity to give of themselves for the sake of the gospel.

Almost overnight, Emma became so physically awkward as a result of her pregnancy that she could hardly go out at all. She became more convinced that her hunch might be well-founded. Her belly seemed far too big to be holding just *one* baby. After supper, she was sitting with her swollen feet up on a chair when Joseph entered the room. He smiled and asked, "Are you as miserable as you look?"

"Most likely." She chuckled, rubbing a hand over her belly. "I feel far too stretched out to grow any more . . . and there are still weeks left to go."

Joseph got a cushion and lifted her feet to put it beneath them, then he sat beside her, putting his hand over hers where their babies grew. "Are you sure there aren't three?" he asked, then put his ear to her belly as if he might hear an answer from inside.

They talked about possible names, speculating over the possibility of two girls, or two boys—or one of each. "Or maybe it's just one very large baby," Emma said, "and my hunch is wrong."

"There's only one way to find out," he said and kissed her. "We'll just have to wait."

Emma's mind went, as it often did, to the experience of giving birth to little Alvin—and then losing him. Going through labor again didn't frighten her nearly as much as her fear of coming through it with no baby to fill her empty arms.

"Hello there, elect lady," Joseph said, touching her chin to tilt her face toward his. "Why the sadness?"

"Is it so obvious?" she asked, shifting her head to his shoulder.

"I'm afraid so."

"More . . . fear, I think; sadness too, perhaps. I was thinking of little Alvin . . . and hoping . . ."

"I understand," he said. "I'm hoping too, Emma—and praying. All the time."

"Then surely everything will be all right," Emma said, wishing she could overcome this nagging fear that it *wouldn't* be. For all her weighing and measuring of thoughts and feelings, she couldn't discern if she was simply paranoid after what had happened before, or if she was being given some kind of warning from the Spirit to prepare her. She could only keep hoping and praying.

Emma's fears assaulted her mercilessly when she went into labor far too early. Even while she fought her way through the accelerating pain, a part of her knew this would end in tragedy. She kept thinking over and over that she would endure any amount of pain to have a child that she could hold and love and nurture. But to live through this to no avail felt cruel and heartless. The midwife was kind and encouraging through the process, but Emma could never tell this sweet woman her deepest fears.

One baby finally came, and then another—a boy and a girl. And as Emma had feared, they did not survive. At first she wept inconsolably, sobbing so hard that it became difficult to catch her breath, which only enhanced the physical pain of her ordeal. Gradually her tears eased into shock, and she lay curled on her side, unable to accept the harsh truth—once again. Enduring pregnancy and childbirth had still left her childless. The emptiness was beyond her ability to grasp. Never had she comprehended such grief! A palpable pain gathered in her chest and threatened to burst out of her, but the shock kept it back, leaving her unable to move, incapable of thinking, barely able to breathe.

"Emma," she heard Joseph whisper and felt his hand on her brow. She only stared at the wall, not wanting to face him with her own inability to give him children. He sat on the edge of the bed and took her hand, which she gave with resistance. A quick glance at his eyes clearly showed his sorrow. She closed her own eyes, unable to bear it.

"Emma," he said again, and with the warm, tender intonations of his voice, perfect love and acceptance came in the simple utterance of her name. She lifted her eyes to meet his, having no doubt that he meant it when he said, "I love you, Emma."

She eased closer to him and tightened her grip on his hand. The pain rushed out of her once again in torrents of sobbing. Still, it felt less painful than holding it inside. And Joseph cried with her. She knew that as long as he was there, as long as she knew he loved her, there was some tiny possibility that she could survive even this.

It quickly became evident to Emma that the pain of this loss was deep, compounded by the death of her first baby. Even with Joseph at her side, sharing her grief, she wondered every hour how she could ever go on. She felt without purpose or meaning when her need to be a mother was paramount. And then Joseph was called away to help console someone else's tragedy, and she was left alone. She slept while he was gone and had no sense of time passing when she awoke to find her husband at her side once again, with a different kind of tears in his eyes.

"Emma," he said as he sat on the edge of the bed and took her hand. It was evident he had news to share. From his expression and the tone of his voice, she couldn't figure out if he was feeling joy or added sorrow, and she wondered what had happened. "Sister Murdock has passed away, Emma," he said, and that answered her question. He was feeling sorrow. "Brother Murdock is overcome with grief." His voice broke, and he pressed a hand to her face. "Oh, Emma! I'm so very grateful that I did not lose *you.*" Sorrow and *gratitude.*

Emma was still trying to take in the news of Sister Murdock's death when Joseph's eyes lit up and fresh tears appeared. But she couldn't identify what he was feeling now. The hint of happiness in his countenance made no sense according to what he'd just told her. "Emma," he said again, this time with more emotion, "Sister Murdock just gave birth to twins—a boy and a girl." Through the long moment it took him to get his composure, Emma's heart began to pound. "Brother Murdock doesn't know what to do, Emma. He can't possibly care for the babies." Joseph let out a shaky laugh that quickly turned to a sob. "I told him that we would take the babies, Emma. And he's agreed. We're to adopt them, raise them as our own."

Emma sucked in her breath, then struggled to let it out. Her immediate response was clouded by hesitancy. The life of one baby could not eradicate the death of another. Emma knew the sorrow she felt over losing her babies would not all at once dissipate simply by caring for someone else's children. But her next thought seemed reassuring and comforting. Sister Murdock's babies could not replace her own, but they could fill the hole of emptiness left by their absence.

"Emma?" Joseph said, bringing her out of her thoughts. "You must tell me if this is what you want. If you—"

"Of course we must take them," she said. How could she leave the babies motherless when such an opportunity lay before her?

She saw Joseph search her eyes with an undefined expectancy, as if he needed to be sure. His own grief over losing their babies was evident in the way he said, "Surely the Lord's hand is in this, Emma." She nodded, too emotional to speak, and once he'd gone to tell Brother Murdock for certain that they would be able to help each other, Emma cried long and hard. She wondered what kind of conversation the two men would share. They were both grieving deeply, but Emma's heart went out to Brother Murdock as she considered that he had lost his wife and now he would be giving up his babies. He had to know there was no other possible way, and she prayed that he would be comforted.

The very moment the infant twins were laid in Emma's arms, their need for her nurturing and care healed something of her aching soul. Her heart opened wider as the love she felt for her three lost infants increased to include these precious children, wiggling and breathing and full of life. How could she not see and acknowledge God's hand in this turn of events, as Joseph had said? Again she felt grief for Brother Murdock's loss, as well as her own, but she rejoiced in being a mother at last.

It took no time at all for Emma to stop seeing the babies as *someone else's children.* Her heart took them in as surely as her arms. Little Joseph and his sister Julia were truly a gift from a merciful Father in Heaven. She felt as if the hollowed-out places in her heart had left room for more joy and appreciation of this great blessing. She treasured every moment as a mother and found her greatest delight in seeing Joseph help care for their children. He was as kind and tender a father as she had expected him to be; much like his own father. With time, Emma determined wholeheartedly that even tragedies could turn into blessings, and she would not trade away her little twins for all the grief she'd endured in order to be prepared to be a mother to them. She felt a deep fulfillment as she recorded their names and the date of their birth in the family Bible. Seeing them written there helped balance the recorded death dates of her own three children. Her hope was restored.

Joseph's mother and other family members arrived in May. They were all so happy to see each other that many tears were shed. Their journey had been long and arduous—even fraught with danger—and they knelt together and thanked God that they had all arrived safely, and that they were reunited as a family. They stayed with Joseph and Emma until Joseph was able to purchase some land for them nearby, and Emma was continually grateful for the comfortable place she'd found in the hearts of Joseph's parents. And it was wonderful to be with Hyrum and Jerusha again. Hyrum's unquestionable love for and support of Joseph was as gratifying for Emma as the sisterhood she found with Jerusha, as well as other members of the family. As they all settled in, Emma allowed herself to begin dreaming once again of finding deep roots in this place, of growing old here with Joseph, raising their children together and being surrounded by loved ones. Ohio was a beautiful place, and it quickly endeared itself to her heart.

According to a pattern that Emma was becoming accustomed to, many marvelous wonders occurred in Kirtland—along with many trials. But the Lord had promised to reveal His law there . . . and He did. The heavens were truly opened in a wonderful way, and Emma rejoiced in their many blessings. The work continued to roll forward, and while missionaries went forth, newcomers kept arriving. As the gathering of Saints grew, Emma realized that her husband drew the attention of many people. Of course, she was more aware than anyone that he was tall and strapping, and undoubtedly handsome. He had a natural charisma that had only been enhanced by the tutelage of angels and the refining process of being a prophet of God. He just had a way of turning heads. It was impossible to pass him on the street and not be aware of something remarkable and unusual about this man.

Those who had come here were naturally curious about the legendary Joseph Smith. Some came with testimonies already firm in their hearts, others with curiosity enough to track down this man who had supposedly translated ancient records and spoken with God and angels. But all who came wanted to meet him, and Emma had to contend with the fact that her husband was a famous man. His humility never waned, and she never had to wonder if she were most important to him. But his mission required him to be a prophet to the people, and she knew that her mission was to share him in that regard. They could hardly step out onto the street without being stopped so that he could answer questions or be introduced to a newcomer—which was far better than being stopped by those who were intent on threatening and harassing him. Either way, he handled each encounter with grace and dignity. Emma did her best to follow his example and remain patient while she heard the same conversations over and over, and as their purposes for being out and about always took much longer than intended. Still, how could she not be pleased, even thrilled, to be the woman at his side?

The twins were not many weeks old when Joseph was called away to Missouri, a place where he'd told her the Lord would build up Zion and great things would occur. Some of the Saints were gathering there, and his leadership was needed. Emma hated being without him, and the more than two months he was gone were lonely and challenging. But she understood the need for it and was determined not to complain. She was greatly blessed to be in her own little home, and she was surrounded by the loving Morley family. And as always, Joseph's family was nearby, offering care and assistance. Upon his return, she treasured his company and enjoyed hearing of every new miracle and revelation that had occurred, and sorrowed over hearing the stories of hardship and persecution that followed her husband—and the Saints.

The twins grew quickly, and life in Kirtland was thriving. But always there was the undercurrent of those opposed to the Mormons and their beliefs. Emma was continually astounded at the ingenuity of Satan in stirring weak-minded people to conjure up all manner of harassment and ill will against people who were simply trying to live their religion in peace. Emma did her best not to worry over such things and kept her focus on the joy of her thriving babies and the social life of those who were gathering in Kirtland.

A day didn't pass without her pondering the revelation the Lord had given to her. Since the Lord had told her "*to expound scriptures, and to exhort the church,*" she prayerfully considered what exactly that meant. She devoted much time to study of the Bible and the Book of Mormon, which was not unusual; she'd grown up studying the Bible, and she'd quickly grown to love and rely on the new volume of scripture that she'd had a tiny part in helping bring forth. But her study took on new depth as she specifically asked for the Spirit's guidance in understanding them better than she ever had. In spite of Joseph's many responsibilities as the leader of a quickly growing church, they often made time to quietly discuss the things they were both learning. Emma's testimony deepened as great principles and doctrines were made very clear to her. She had not seen any visions or heard voices, but the Spirit taught her just as plainly. Through her growing knowledge, she occasionally found opportunity to converse with new members who were struggling to understand gospel truths, or those who were curious—or even cynical. Prayerfully trying to be bold without being overbearing, more often than not she was able to offer some perspective that brought about good results. Emma found fulfillment in being able to make such contributions, even if they were tiny in comparison to the grand sermons her husband preached and the reputation he was gaining. Still, she knew she was doing the Lord's will in her own quiet way, and it brought her much joy.

Emma also continued to work on gathering the hymns, as the Lord had instructed, and to do all else He'd asked of her to support her husband in his ministry. In her youth she never would have imagined herself as the wife of a great religious leader, but putting the pieces of her life together, she could see now that it was her calling to stand by Joseph's side, as much as it was *his* calling to restore the gospel of Jesus Christ to the earth. She couldn't imagine a more difficult life at times, nor could she imagine one more fulfilling.

Emma never doubted for a moment that her husband's calling was divine, and that his authority and power were indeed from God. But there were moments when even she was taken aback by this reality. At one of the many meetings held in their home, Emma felt mildly disinterested in the conversation that focused on speculation over supernatural gifts of healing, such as those that had existed in the days of Jesus' Apostles. One of the men present stated somewhat flippantly, while pointing to a woman in the room, "Here is Mrs. Johnson with a lame arm; has God given any power to men now on the earth to cure her?"

The conversation went in another direction, and Emma had forgotten about the comment until Joseph stood up, took Mrs. Johnson by the hand and commanded her, in the name of Jesus Christ, to be healed. He walked out of the room, leaving stunned silence in his absence. Emma felt sure that some of those present might consider such bold action to be some kind of joke. But immediately Mrs. Johnson lifted up her arm—and it was healed.

After their guests had all left and the house was quiet, Emma sat brushing out her hair, pondering the miracle she had witnessed. She marveled that the same man who slept by her side and helped care for their babies had the power of God in him sufficient to perform miracles too wondrous to comprehend. Then he walked into the room and sat on the edge of the bed to remove his boots. Emma was wondering how to express her thoughts without trivializing the experience. Then she felt him take the brush from her hand, moving it through her hair in long, even strokes, pressing his other hand over the trail of the brush each time.

"I love you, Emma," he said, and she momentarily closed her eyes to more fully absorb his words—and their meaning—into her spirit. Before she could respond, he set the brush aside and knelt in front of her. The genuine humility and affection in his eyes only contributed to her wonder over what she knew him to be capable of as a prophet of God.

Emma took his hands into hers. She rubbed her thumbs over the callouses that were evidence of the hard work he did. He was as adept at laboring side by side with the Saints as he was in dictating revelations and preaching grand sermons of gospel truths. She pressed his hands to the sides of her face and again closed her eyes.

"How does it feel?" she asked in a voice of reverence.

"What?" he asked, confused.

"When you heal someone," she clarified.

"The Lord heals. I am only the—"

"I know," she said and opened her eyes to meet his. "But . . . how does it feel?"

He thought about it a moment. His voice was hushed. "It feels . . . warm; I feel warmth in my hands."

Emma pressed them more tightly to her face. "I am truly blessed . . . to share my life with such a remarkable man."

She saw doubt in his eyes. He shook his head slightly. "I don't *feel* remarkable, Emma. I'm just . . . an ordinary man . . . trying to do what God requires of me. Sometimes I feel so . . . unequal to my charge. I wonder . . . how could He have chosen *me?*"

Emma smiled. While she didn't want him to be weighed down by such self-doubt, it was reassuring to know that he struggled with it at times, the same way she did. "Because you're remarkable," she said. "God doesn't require you to be perfect, Joseph; no man is. I think you're doing just fine."

He drew a deep breath, as if he were taking her words into his spirit. "You keep telling me that," he said and wrapped his arms around her, laying his head against her shoulder. Emma pressed her fingers into his hair, savoring the moment. Such quiet togetherness was precious to her.

"I will!" she said eagerly. "Oh, and . . . by the way . . . I love you, Joseph Smith—not because you're remarkable. But just because I do." She laughed softly. "Being remarkable doesn't hurt any, however."

"What I really wonder," he said, picking up on her lightened mood, "is how I captured the heart of such a *remarkable* woman." He came to his feet and lifted her into his arms, sitting in her seat in order to hold her on his lap.

"I think it was your singing ability," she said, and he laughed.

Joseph laughed again, and she wrapped her arms around his neck. "And I thought you were a woman of integrity, Emma."

"Oh, I am! What I meant was . . . that you needed *me* to teach you how to sing . . . and therefore you captured my heart."

"I can agree with that," he said. "But you forgot to mention that I can never keep up with you on horseback. How can I not feel honored to be in the presence of such a woman?"

Emma gave him a sidelong glance and a skeptical chuckle. "It is the other way around, I can assure you."

Joseph became more serious, shaking his head slightly. His eyes brimmed with such overt admiration that Emma was nearly moved to tears. How could a woman not feel valuable when such a fine man looked at her that way? "I have always been—and forever will be—in awe of you . . . Emma Smith." And then he kissed her.

Emma was pleased—and not surprised—to learn that the healing of Mrs. Johnson's hand had not been temporary. The Johnsons soon became members of the Church—and no wonder, Emma thought with pleasure at the announcement that they would be baptized. Joseph and Emma talked it over and felt good about accepting the Johnsons' invitation to stay in their home in Hiram while Joseph worked on translating certain passages of the Bible that were incorrect. While Joseph and Sidney Rigdon were committed to the work, Emma helped Sister Johnson with household duties and found joy in caring for her babies. She always felt more at ease when Joseph's work kept him close to home, and she enjoyed his presence there, even though he was terribly busy. Their work continued through the winter, and it was a time of contentment for Emma. More heavenly manifestations occurred, and she felt reverent amazement as Joseph shared the details with her during quiet moments.

In March of 1832, when the twins were about eleven months old, they both contracted the measles. Emma and Joseph couldn't help fearing the worst with such a dreadful ailment, and Emma could only care for her babies the best she knew how and pray that they would come through all right. But fear combined forces with fatigue and left her struggling just to keep her bearings. It was difficult to remember to have faith when one baby or the other—or both—were wailing in misery much of the time.

With two sick babies, Emma accomplished nothing through the course of a long day beyond struggling to keep them content. Sister Johnson helped some, but she had other things to attend to, and Emma was simply grateful to have someone else running the household so that she could focus on the babies' needs. Little Joseph's illness grew worse, and his fussing was more severe than Julia's, but his need for constant attention did not alleviate Julia's need for care as well. As always, when Joseph was able to help, it eased much of Emma's strain. He walked the floor with little Joseph long after supper was over, while Emma cuddled Julia in the rocking chair. As her little girl finally stopped fussing and relaxed, Emma did the same. She drifted in and out of sleep, aware of little Joseph's continued fussing. Then it became quiet, and she opened her eyes long enough to see Joseph get into bed, placing their son beside him, sound asleep. It only took Emma another minute to fall back to sleep herself, praying as she did that the babies' illness would soon relent.

Emma came out of sleep so abruptly that her heart was pounding with fear before she even realized her home had been invaded. In the space of a breath, the babies started screaming, their cries sharply mingled with Joseph's protests as he was dragged out of bed. Emma shrieked, barely awake enough to be convinced that more men than she could count were carrying her husband out of the house, issuing threats that strangled Emma's heart with the fear that he would not come back alive. She clutched Julia against her and screamed Joseph's name from the open doorway, as if doing so might stop this madness. A part of her wanted to run after them, to be with her husband, no matter what might happen. But her deeper instincts reminded her of the need to protect her children and to keep herself from harm. If something happened to her, who would care for them? She scrambled to find little Joseph and fought to calm the babies down. She wondered where Brother and Sister Johnson were, and feared something terrible was happening to them, as well. From a distance she could hear the shouting and swearing of these horrible men, but the din did not muffle the sound of Joseph crying out in pain. "No!" Emma cried and pressed herself against the invisible barrier that kept her from rushing to his side. She paced the floor with one baby in her arms, then the other—sometimes both, crying tears that did not begin to express her fear and horror. Her stomach hurt, twisted into knots as it was. Her heart pounded with such a harsh rhythm that her breathing could barely keep up. The reality felt impossible to believe. How could it have come to this? How much would they—most especially Joseph—be required to suffer for this cause? And worst of all, she had to wonder if this was the end for him. Had fears she'd been too afraid to hardly consider come to pass? Yet, for all the persecution they had faced, her mind could have never conceived of something so appalling as this. What manner of men would do such a thing? For all her exposure to mob violence, she had never encountered such evil.

Finally the babies slept, and Emma carefully hid them, fearing these despicable men might return and do harm to them all. She continued to pace, crying, praying aloud, fighting the fear in her heart. "Please bring him home to me," she uttered over and over. "I will do whatever you require of me, Lord, just . . . please bring him home."

Considering the possibilities of what torture might be inflicted on Joseph, Emma wondered for a moment if it might be better for him if he were *not* spared. But she quickly squelched the very idea; living without him was unthinkable. She *needed* him. The *Saints* needed him. Surely his work was far from finished. She prayed on and on, wondering if she would have no choice but to leave her babies and go searching for him. Instead she searched out Brother and Sister Johnson and found them barricaded in their room, but gratefully they were unharmed. Together they watched, waited, and wondered—praying and fighting the urge to go and search for Joseph. For all their desire to help him, they all agreed that any aggressive action would only see them harmed as well, and it would likely do Joseph no good either.

Hours after Joseph had been taken away, Emma saw him through the darkness, staggering toward the house. She heard him call for a blanket, and then he came into view, his head and body so covered in blood she couldn't recognize him. She was so horrified that everything went black.

Emma's next awareness was Sister Johnson gently urging her back into consciousness. Remembering what had preceded her fainting, Emma gasped for breath and cried out Joseph's name, resisting Sister Johnson's efforts to keep her down until she felt more steady. When she saw her husband and took in the reality of what had happened to him, only a miracle kept her from fainting again. What she had believed to be blood was in fact tar. The mob had stripped the clothing off her husband and covered him with tar, but not before they'd beaten and tried to poison him. And to complete the unspeakable degradation of their act, they had scattered feathers into the tar. His tooth was chipped, his body battered, and his skin burned from the natural acid in the tar. Emma hadn't been any more upset over the deaths of her babies. Even in that moment, a part of her knew this would likely be the worst experience of their lives; or perhaps she only hoped it would be. How could anything *ever* be worse than this?

Emma was grateful at least for the kindness of Brother and Sister Johnson. Without their help, she never would have been able to deal with her fussing babies and still be able to help Joseph on her own. It took most of the night to remove the tar—an excruciating process that often took hair or skin with it as it came off. Emma could hardly stop crying, and she made it clear to Joseph how much she hated the men who had done this to him.

Even in such pain, and tortured as he was, Joseph responded with sincerity, "I understand, Emma, but . . . we have to let hate go."

"How do we do that?" she asked, wiping her tears with her sleeve while she continued to pick feathers and the horrible sticky blackness from his hair. But at least she could see his face now, bruised and bleeding as it was.

Joseph grimaced and struggled for composure. He hesitated but was not lacking in conviction as he said with a halting voice, "Like every other burden, we bring it to the Lord . . . and leave it with Him."

Emma said nothing. She knew that was the correct Christian attitude, and she knew that no man was a better Christian than her husband. But it was going to take some time for her to come to terms with following his example of forgiveness in this case. He grimaced and moaned as she carefully peeled tar from his back, fighting the steady stream of tears on her face.

"Perhaps . . . I am meant to swim in deep waters," he muttered and grimaced again.

Emma sobbed and kept working, desperately needing to remove every bit of the dreadful, black residue from his skin and hair, as if doing so might erase the horror.

"We can be grateful, at least," Joseph added a minute later, "that I have survived this . . . to continue the Lord's work."

"Yes, I *am* grateful for that," she admitted, knowing her prayers on that account had been answered. But she wondered what else they might have to suffer in order for him to continue the Lord's work.

Once Joseph was free of the tar, they both tried to get some rest, but Emma knew that he could hardly relax because of all the pain he was in. Later in the day she found him struggling to get dressed. While he wasn't aware of her presence, she watched him pull his suspenders up over his shoulders, wincing with every move.

"What *are* you doing?" she demanded, startling him.

"I have to give that sermon today; you know I do. It's the Sabbath." He sat down gingerly and lowered his head, as if he were fighting to get his equilibrium.

"You were nearly *killed* last night, Joseph," she said as if he might have forgotten. "You're in no condition to do this."

"I must, Emma," he pleaded, even while he was close to tears from the pain he was enduring. His chipped tooth had affected the way he talked, and Emma was still trying to get used to it. She hated what would become the constant reminder of what had happened. "I must let the people see that I will not be thwarted in doing the Lord's work. I want the men who did this to . . ." He squeezed his eyes closed and swallowed hard. "I want them . . . to know that . . . they did not succeed . . . that I will not let their hatred . . . make me waver."

"Oh, Joseph," she said more softly, sitting beside him. "Your faith inspires me."

She took his hand, and he carefully laid his head on her shoulder. She felt tortured by the evidence of how every move he made was painful. "There are times," he said with a catch in his voice, "when there is . . . nothing but faith . . . to hold on to. But I must hold on."

"Very well," she said, "but I'm not letting you out of my sight."

"You take very good care of me, Sister Smith," he said.

Joseph rose carefully to his feet, and Emma wasn't certain how exactly to help; she was nearly afraid to touch him, knowing that much of his skin was burned or raw. Once he was standing, she held his coat for him and watched as he gingerly slipped his arms into the sleeves.

"I'm going to need your help with my tie," he said, motioning toward it.

Emma picked up the tie and wrapped it around the high collar of his shirt. While she was efficiently tying it into the proper knot, she muttered just for the sake of it, "I still can't believe you're going to preach in this condition." She sighed and fought back tears. "I hate those men for what they did to you, Joseph. I know we have to let it go, just as you said, but . . . maybe I don't have as much faith as you do."

"I know *that's* not true," he said. Their eyes met, and she saw tears well up in his at the same moment they burned into her own. "I love you, Emma," he said. "Everything will be all right. We just . . . have to let go."

"You keep telling me that," she said and carefully straightened his tie.

A short while later Emma sat listening to Joseph's words as he stood in the doorway of the Johnson home and spoke to the crowd. He stood tall and firm, in spite of what he'd endured the night before. The physical evidence of his persecution was blatantly evident on his face, and he held tightly to the back of a chair to keep himself standing. But as he bore witness of Jesus Christ, and the power of His atoning sacrifice, Emma's heart found a tiny measure of hope that she *could* let go of what the hand of hate had done to her precious Joseph. It was evident that those listening to him speak were deeply moved. How could they not be touched by such an example, when Emma certainly was? And Emma knew that if Joseph could let go of hate and give it to the Lord, she needed to do so as well.

Once Joseph had fulfilled his obligation of appearing in public, the trauma of his tarring was overshadowed by the worsening of their son's illness. While Julia showed improvement, little Joseph's symptoms gave them cause for great concern. Emma's feelings over the matter were made more difficult because she *knew* that the baby's exposure to the cold the previous night during the commotion of his father being dragged out of the house was the greatest factor in his worsening illness. Her prayers to come to terms with her anger and hatred were sharply mingled with her prayers that little Joseph would get better. But the child's condition only deteriorated, and just a few days after the hateful mob had invaded their home, Emma's flailing hope was shattered as their son died in her arms.

CHAPTER EIGHT

Song of the Heart

Emma rocked Joseph's lifeless little body in her arms, sobbing with painful heaves that didn't begin to release her agony. Joseph knelt on the floor beside her, wrapping her in his arms. He pressed his face into her hair and wept. Minutes crept into hours with nothing to say to each other until Julia needed her mother's attention. Joseph left to once again build a little pine box in which to lay another of their children to rest.

Emma found some tiny measure of comfort in thinking that little Joseph was now reunited with the mother who had given birth to him. But even that knowledge could not compensate for the fact that Emma had now seen four of her babies buried.

Little Joseph was barely in the ground before Joseph was required to leave for Missouri on Church business. Worried over the well-being of Emma and little Julia, Joseph wrote Emma a letter, telling her that arrangements had been made for her to return to Kirtland and stay with Sister Whitney while he was away. But a breakdown in communication left Emma utterly reliant on the charity of others to house and feed her and her daughter.

Joseph's family did what they could to help, but their own space and resources were limited. For months Emma felt little better than a gypsy, going from house to house and suffering the ill effects of another pregnancy. The discovery that she would have another baby was wrought with such a mixture of emotions that it was difficult to sift through them enough to find the joy. If she could believe that the child growing inside of her might actually live to be an adult, nothing could make her happier. But given her present situation, she could hardly even ponder the possibility. Wondering every day if her husband was all right, she could only think of him and do all she could to see that Julia remained safe and healthy. She didn't have time to think about being pregnant, even if the symptoms were a continual reminder.

After what seemed forever, Joseph was finally able to return. Emma's joy at being reunited with him was beyond her ability to express in words. He quickly found better living arrangements for them, which alleviated many of her concerns. A three-room apartment above the Whitney Store served as their home, the Church office, and the School of the Prophets, and Emma served many boarders while living there. Joseph continued to be gone much of the time; as the work expanded, he was called away more and more, and Emma was often left on her own to handle daily matters. But she felt the Lord sustaining her, even as she recounted all they had survived and risen above. With Joseph back in her life and with their situation feeling more secure and stable, Emma's acceptance and hope in regard to her pregnancy also blossomed.

While Joseph came and went, the city of Kirtland grew and thrived. In fact, it grew so quickly with Saints continually arriving that Joseph and Emma often gave up their own bed to help accommodate the newcomers. But those were days Emma cherished. The Church was flourishing, and she and Joseph were happy working together and anticipating the birth of another baby. Each day they prayed together that it would be born healthy and strong, and Emma chose not to think of any other possibility. Julia was precious to her beyond measure. Still, she longed for another child. A new baby could not take the place of those she had lost, but she felt certain it would help fill the hole created by their absence.

Many kinds of meetings were typically held in their home, and Emma grew accustomed to Church leaders and members coming and going for any number of reasons. One sunny afternoon, Joseph and the brethren who comprised the leadership of the Church became engaged in a lengthy meeting. While Julia napped, Emma took advantage of the time to work on the ongoing project of gathering and transcribing appropriate hymns. The work required for such an undertaking had proven to be much more than she'd anticipated, especially with having to fit it in along with the regular tasks of everyday living that were often taxing in and of themselves. Still, little by little it was coming together, and she felt confident that when the time was right it would be completed, and the combination of hymns would be a great contribution to the Saints.

Occasionally Emma would smile when she heard a burst of laughter from the other room where the men were gathered. But mostly there were long stretches of silence, and she wondered what they might be discussing. Waiting and wondering were common aspects of her life, but she chose not to let it dampen her mood. It was simply the way it had to be. When she stopped to ponder the responsibilities on Joseph's shoulders, she wondered how he even managed to make it from day to day. And yet he always pressed forward with zeal and commitment to his purpose. How could she not be inspired by his example?

While copying down the lyrics to a hymn she dearly loved, Emma hummed the melody and paused to check her spelling. The door opened, and Joseph emerged from the meeting, along with the other brethren. After they'd all left, Joseph sat across from her and announced wih hushed reverence that, under the direction of the Lord, they would be building a temple.

"A temple?" she echoed, as if she'd never heard the word.

"A temple, yes," he said with that prophetic glow in his eyes, "not unlike those in biblical times."

"I see," Emma said, wondering what exactly the construction of a temple would entail. She couldn't even imagine, since she had very little idea of what a temple might actually be like. Surely it was meant to be grand and elaborate, which seemed ludicrous considering how many of the Saints were just trying to build simple homes in order to have a roof over their heads. *A temple.* The idea settled comfortably into her spirit in spite of how foreign it felt.

Later that evening, after Julia was down for the night, Emma sat on the edge of the bed to brush out her hair. Joseph laid close beside her, and with a familiar faraway glow in his eyes, he told her in astounding detail about the temple they would build. Apparently God would now guide him through becoming an architect, as well as a translator of ancient records. Emma didn't fully understand the purpose or importance of the temple, but she knew that Joseph did. She could see a distinct light in his eyes as he spoke of having the great structure in their midst, and the wondrous blessings that would come because of it. The hope she felt in the air around them was amplified when she felt the baby moving inside of her. It wasn't difficult to imagine growing old together in this place with Joseph and their children—and a temple.

Emma was not at all pleased when, as she was approaching the end of her pregnancy, Joseph had to leave on Church business.

"What if you don't make it back before the baby comes?" she asked, not wanting to sound whiny, but needing to share her concerns.

He offered a wan smile and put a hand to her face. "I will do everything I can to get back as soon as possible." He pressed a lingering kiss to her brow. "You are in my heart and in my prayers . . . always."

"I know," she said, preferring not to cry but unable to hold back. She took hold of his upper arms and put her head to his shoulder. "I'm just so . . . afraid. What if . . ."

"You don't have to say it, Emma. I admit that I share your fears, but we must trust in the Lord . . . and do the best that we can." He drew back to look into her eyes. "Surely He will take good care of you while I'm gone." Emma nodded stoutly and swallowed the temptation to sob. "I love you, Emma," he added, and the temptation became more difficult to resist.

"I love you too, Joseph," she said, her voice cracking. He kissed her and had to leave.

Once Emma had vented her emotions with a good, long cry, she resigned herself to doing as Joseph had admonished: trust in the Lord and do the best that she could. In his absence she was especially grateful to be near his family. Hyrum's wife, Jerusha, was good company, and Emma's closeness to Joseph's parents deepened as they came to rely on each other more and more. Their bonds as a family were amplified by their absolute knowledge that Joseph had been called by God, and by their mutual commitment to remain anxiously engaged in doing whatever God required.

On a cold November day, Emma's heart fell when her labor started and Joseph had not returned. But Joseph's mother stayed with her every minute. Lucy did well at encouraging Emma through the pain and offering hope that the baby would be all right. Emma's previous childbirth experiences made it difficult to take hold of such hope, even while a part of her desperately ached for it to be so. To hold a living, healthy baby in her arms seemed the greatest miracle possible at that point in time.

When Lucy placed the wiggling little boy in Emma's arms, she allowed herself to feel a measure of reserved joy. She kept watching him closely, fearing she might see some sign that he wasn't healthy, that he might not hold on. But it quickly became evident that he was a perfect little boy, that he would live. Emma's joy was beyond her ability to express. She held her infant son close to her face and wept tears of relief and gladness. She only wished that Joseph could be there to share in the moment. As it was, she shared the experience with her son, singing to him in a lilting voice one of her favorite hymns that more resembled a lullaby. *A song of the heart is a prayer unto God,* she thought, recalling words from the revelation that had been given to her. In that moment her heart was full of inexpressible gratitude, but she felt certain God knew and understood as she sang the deepest praise in her heart.

Emma's mind was drawn to the first baby she'd lost, and how her mother had been with her. She wished that her mother could have been here now, to see this beautiful boy and share in her happiness. As it was, she could only pray that her parents were well—as she did each and every day—and that somehow, some way, their hearts would soften.

Soon after the birth, Emma's heart quickened to hear the familiar sound of Joseph's boots hurrying up the stairs, then his voice just outside the open door, speaking to his mother.

"Is she . . ." he began.

"Everything's fine," Lucy replied with a catch in her voice, then Joseph entered the room.

He rushed to Emma's side, sitting on the edge of the bed to hold her close, laughing as he uttered her name and pressed his face into her hair. "You're all right?" he asked, taking her face into his hands. Emma nodded, too emotional to speak. Joseph turned when his mother appeared at his side, and Emma heard him gasp as he took in the fact that she held a blanketed bundle in her arms—and she was smiling. "You have a perfect . . . beautiful . . . healthy son," Lucy said, placing the baby into Joseph's large hands.

He glanced at Emma with a happiness that filled her soul. His gaze focused on the baby, and his entire countenance brightened. She wondered if the joy of being a father might be in the same realm as visions and revelations. It seemed so by the glow in his face.

"I think we should call him Joseph," Emma suggested, "like his father . . . and grandfather."

"I think it's perfect," Joseph said. "It would be an honor to share my name with such a fine boy." He chuckled softly in response to the baby's sweet little noises.

Once again they had a little Joseph in their home, and Emma had never felt happier. Julia loved her new brother, and their little family became even closer as they worked together to care for the baby. Extended family also found much happiness with this newest arrival, and Emma's hopes for a bright future became easier to hold on to.

Not long after the birth of little Joseph, a man by the name of Brigham Young came to Kirtland, intent on meeting the famed Joseph Smith. He'd known before his arrival that he would be meeting a prophet. He and his wife had joined the Church in New York, and she had died only a few weeks before he'd left to come to Kirtland. Being a widower with two young children, the gospel had given him much hope and strength. Many came to Kirtland, some with varying degrees of curiosity and skepticism, but Joseph told Emma that Brigham was a unique man who would prove significant to the Lord's work. And she believed him.

While Emma watched her children growing, plans for the temple solidified and construction began. It seemed a grand undertaking, but Emma had complete faith in whatever Joseph's vision might entail. As the temple rose, many miracles occurred. The work was hard, however, and required much sacrifice on behalf of the Saints. Many faithfully endured, no matter what hardship they were called to face, while others fell away, becoming bitter and angry. Still, no amount of opposition kept the work from moving forward. An official First Presidency was sustained, and revelation continued to come from the Lord. Joseph came and went, always with one problem or another to solve, but almost always remaining in good spirits. Emma knew more than anyone the joy he felt in all the good that was coming to pass. She also knew more than anyone how the welfare of the Saints weighed heavily upon him. His hopes for Zion being established in Missouri were sometimes difficult to hold onto when they heard of mob violence and persecution. When word came that Saints had been driven from their homes, Joseph became wracked with grief and spent much time in earnest prayer. Emma didn't know how to console him. She could give no advice but to trust in the Lord and follow His counsel. Even though Joseph already knew that, it seemed at times he needed to hear her say it. And often he just needed her to listen while he verbalized the problems.

Joseph and Emma were thrilled when Brigham married Mary Ann Angel, a kind and gentle woman who became a mother to his two children. Emma deeply appreciated Brigham's support of Joseph's work, and was grateful to find a new friend in Mary Ann.

Emma was quite accustomed to Joseph leaving home to attend to Church business, but when he left early in May with a company of two hundred men, she felt near despair. The purpose of their journey was to aid the suffering Saints in Missouri who had been driven from their homes, and to take back their confiscated property. They were going with the understanding that a fight would be imminent, and that their lives could be in danger. As always, Emma fought to put her trust in the Lord to see her husband—and those with him—safely returned home. Joseph was continually in her prayers, while she was kept far too busy attending to her children and the responsibilities left to her in Joseph's absence. She knew that others looked to her as an example—a fact that was somewhat disconcerting. But she did her best to live as she believed God wanted her to live, and hoped that she wouldn't let the Saints down.

While Joseph was gone, a newspaper published an article claiming that he was dead. Emma became distraught and grieved for the loss of her husband each waking moment until she received evidence that it had been only a false rumor. And then she had to contend with her feelings of anger at having to experience such grief due to vicious gossip.

When Joseph returned from Missouri, she was inexplicably grateful to hold him in her arms. His happiness at seeing her and the children gave her perfect joy. She knew even before he told her that the journey had been difficult, and there were many challenges weighing on him. But Emma found consolation in being able to share his burdens. He spoke of the dissension and murmuring among the men, and how the purpose of their journey had been much different than any of them had expected.

"But the Lord's purposes have been served, Emma," he said, holding both her hands in his while they sat close together and talked into the night. "I have no doubt that the men who remained faithful through this experience will yet do great things to build the kingdom of God."

Joseph's concerns for the people of Missouri continued, but Emma encouraged him to do as he had taught *her*—to do all that was in his power and then trust in the Lord.

Joseph's parents were equally glad for his return. As always, they were continually involved and supportive. Emma treasured her closeness to Lucy, which made up somewhat for the absence of her own mother, even if she never stopped missing her parents or wondering how they were. And Joseph's father was dear to Emma. Like Lucy, he helped compensate for the loss of her own parents in her life. When Joseph, Sr., was called to be the Patriarch of the Church, it felt fitting and right that he should hold that calling. But the rightness of it touched Emma deeply when her father-in-law gave her a patriarchal blessing. Like the revelation given through Joseph years earlier, it became a source of comfort and strength to Emma.

In the blessing, Emma was told many great and marvelous things that let her know beyond any doubt the blessing did indeed come from God. No one else could have wholly known her heart as He did. While every word of the blessing was precious to her, certain principles of what she was told especially touched her heart and gave her hope as she referred back to them over and over . . . *Thou art blessed of the Lord, for thy faithfulness and truth, thou shalt be blessed with thy husband, and rejoice in the glory which shall come upon him.*

Thy soul has been afflicted because of the wickedness of men in seeking the destruction of thy companion, and thy whole soul has been drawn out in prayer for his deliverance; rejoice, for the Lord thy God has heard thy supplications. Thou has grieved for the hardness of the hearts of thy father's house, and thou has longed for their salvation. The Lord will have respect to thy cries . . .

Thou shalt see many days, yea, the Lord will spare thee till thou art satisfied, for thou shalt see thy Redeemer. Thy heart shalt rejoice in the great work of the Lord, and no one shall take thy rejoicing from thee . . . Thou has seen much sorrow because the Lord has taken from thee three of thy children. In this thou art not to be blamed, for he knows thy pure desires to raise up a family . . . The holy angels shall watch over thee and thou shalt be saved in the kingdom of God . . .

Emma often pondered her blessing and prayed to understand its deepest meaning, and she continued to do the same in regard to the revelation that had been given to her much earlier. From them both she was able to glean strength and guidance in order to press forward in doing all that God required of her—whatever that might be. Knowing that God was mindful of her struggles and that His love for her was strong and true added to her growing contentment. Life in Kirtland was good, despite the ongoing and distressing presence of opposition that continually made it evident that Satan would zealously tempt the hearts of men to attempt to hold back the work of God. Opposition had always been a part of their lives, but it became especially difficult for Joseph—and for Emma—when members of the Church fell away, and even some who were closest to them began to murmur and cause dissension. Joseph's leadership was challenged, and libelous literature filled with all manner of hideous lies and distortions regarding Mormonism began to circulate. Emma found it difficult not to feel angry over such matters, especially when they affected Joseph—and subsequently her—so personally. But her husband's example always guided her to earnest prayer and humility. Sometimes she wished that all who knew him—friends and enemies alike—could see the side to him that she could see. His sincere desire to do God's will, mingled with his own human struggle to do so, was as endearing as it was inspiring. But in truth, Emma was grateful to carry the exclusive privilege of knowing him as no one did.

Despite the continuing struggles and hardships, Emma derived happiness and fulfillment as she observed the growth and progress of the Church, as well as that of her own little family. Julia and little Joseph were strong and healthy, and they were a source of much joy to their parents, as well as to all who knew them. Her own life was made more pleasant by their move to a two-story frame house down the hill from the temple, not far from the Chagrin River.

It was a grand step for Joseph when twelve Apostles were chosen, as well as a group of seventy men who would lead and guide the Church under the prophet's direction. All but a few of these men had faithfully endured the hardships of the arduous journey to Zion with Joseph, and Emma's faith was strengthened to witness this marvelous example of how the Lord prepares His people in ways that are at times impossible to see from a mortal perspective. Emma could look around at the hardships being endured by many of the Saints and wonder what the Lord might be preparing each individual to accomplish; she also looked at her own life and wondered the same.

Time passed speedily on, and the growth of the Church was evidenced by the need to reprint the Book of Mormon. Continuing missionary efforts were spreading the gospel rapidly, and the temple continued to rise. The sacrifice of the people in regard to these accomplishments was wondrous to behold, and often caused Emma to reflect humbly on being privileged enough to be at the center of such efforts. In spite of ongoing challenges, Emma felt happy and secure. She loved being a mother as well as being an active participant in the events surrounding her husband's mission. He'd been born to this work, and she had been born to stand beside him.

Emma took many opportunities to interact with the residents of Kirtland and its surrounding areas, some who were members of the Church and some who were not. It was common for her to spend her time and resources assisting those who were just arriving, or in helping those who faced varying degrees of illness or hardship. Despite the skeptics and disbelievers, Emma had no trouble being bold enough to defend her husband. And her testimony of the truthfulness of all he taught was something she shared eagerly. Occasionally she would see the softening of hearts through her influence as she helped others understand that what they might initially view as strange and unseemly actually lent validity and divine logic to the nature of the Restoration. Some criticized Joseph for what they called behavior inappropriate for a prophet. But Emma took every opportunity to point out that it was a truly great man who would run through the streets with boys who looked up to him, if only to let them know that he cared about them enough to do so.

Some of the men teased Joseph for doing menial household chores, but Emma could almost guess that he considered hanging the wash or beating a rug—out in the open for others to see—a sound example he expected other men to follow. He worked side by side with many people, often stopping long enough to play stick-pull or answer gospel questions. In time, many who were initially skeptical about the possibility of God speaking to a fourteen-year-old boy were able to realize God's wisdom in speaking to someone who was young and tender enough to listen. Joseph was loved and admired on every side—barring those ever-present detractors who would do him ill. It was impossible to truly know him and see how he behaved toward his fellow men without knowing that something about him was good and right. He lived what he taught, and Emma loved him for it.

While Joseph shared much with Emma about the progress of his work and the happenings of the Church, time and circumstances did not allow for him to share everything. Long talks were a luxury that occurred far too rarely. Still, she sensed his burdens. There were some things she felt sure he *couldn't* share with her, for the sake of confidentiality. Or perhaps he was trying to protect her from things that would only cause her worry and concern. She didn't press him on such matters; she only wished there was more she could do to calm his concerns and ease his burdens.

Emma continued her work on the collection of hymns, carefully choosing those that would give the Saints an opportunity to express their praise to God through song. Some were well-established pieces that were familiar among all Christians. Many of them were new compositions, specifically adapted to their faith and the restoration of the gospel. The process of searching out and compiling the hymns had been challenging at times, and it was an enormous amount of work. But Emma had felt the guidance of the Spirit in her holy commission, and seeing the book ready to go to the printer was especially fulfilling. As the temple neared its completion, Emma was thrilled to know that the hymnal would be ready in time for the dedicatory service. Her joy was added upon with the discovery that she was pregnant once again. She prayed that all would go well again this time, and that they would be able to continue adding to their little family.

Emma was with Joseph at the Whitney store when Hyrum walked in, carrying a box of the printed hymn books. She emitted a spontaneous burst of excited laughter that made Joseph chuckle as he took one from the top of the box and proudly handed it to Emma. The book was tiny due to the scarcity of paper, but just seeing it in print made her heart swell.

"Oh, it's lovely!" Emma said.

"It is indeed," Joseph commented while they both thumbed through separate copies.

"And perhaps," Hyrum said, "its size will make it easier for people to carry it around and keep it close."

"Always finding blessings in the challenges," Joseph said with a sideways smile toward his brother, then he focused on Emma. "You did it," he said warmly. "And you did it so well."

Emma said nothing. If she attempted to speak, surely she would end up spilling all of the gratitude presently overflowing from her heart, along with copious tears. Her fulfillment was more than doubled in seeing the book of Doctrine and Covenants, a collection of Joseph's revelations from the Lord, which had been published alongside the hymn book.

Later that evening, when supper was over, Emma found Joseph carefully perusing the little hymn book. Sitting beside him, she was reminded of the day she'd first held a copy of the Book of Mormon in her hands. While she knew her little book of songs would not carry nearly the significance as translated scripture, she also knew that the words printed between its covers would gladden hearts and strengthen testimonies. She knew its importance to God because she had felt His hand guiding her in the work ever since she had been asked to compile the hymns in the revelation Joseph had received.

After the children were ready for bed, Joseph gathered them close to him on the bed to spend some quiet minutes with them.

Little Joseph was now three and a half, and Julia was almost five. This was Emma's favorite time of day, especially when Joseph was at home. They would sing and pray together, and Joseph would ask the children questions and talk to them in ways that reminded Emma of why she loved him so dearly.

Emma especially loved to hear him speak of the visions he'd had, and the hope it gave him in being reunited one day with loved ones who had passed on. For Joseph, being able to see his brother Alvin again gave him great comfort and joy.

Joseph put an arm around each of the children and drew them close. His voice took on a tremor of emotion. "Did you know that when I was a child, I didn't believe that such a great miracle might be possible? Can you imagine, children, how wondrous it might be to see all of our loved ones again in heaven? Isn't it marvelous to know that they are not lost?"

Emma thought of her own family members and prayed that such a miracle might be possible for them. She exchanged a warm smile with her husband and eased closer to be included in their little circle. The children shifted to allow room for her head on Joseph's shoulder. She heard him whisper, "I love you, Emma," before he pressed a kiss in front of her ear. Emma rubbed a hand over her swollen belly, feeling added joy in the prospect of sharing another child with this wonderful man who held her heart. Surely life could be no better than this!

The dedication service for the temple was the realization of many blessings for the faithful Saints—and especially for Joseph and Emma. The heavens were truly opened that day, and miracles occurred that were witnessed by many. It was surely one of the greatest days of their lives, and Emma concluded that every trial and tribulation endured had been worth the honor of being part of an event with such eternal consequence. She felt certain it was a day that would be recorded in history and spoken of for many generations.

One of the highlights for Emma was hearing her husband offer the dedicatory prayer. When he spoke with such presence and authority, there was no denying that he was a prophet of God. In such moments it was sometimes difficult to comprehend that he was her husband, her soul mate, her dearest friend. And she knew he felt the same about her. She was truly blessed among women!

The words of the prayer were eloquent and profound, laced with prophecy and accompanied by an outpouring of the Spirit. Emma felt especially touched when she heard Joseph say, *"Lord, remember thy servant, Joseph Smith, Junior, and all his afflictions and persecutions—how he has covenanted with Jehovah, and vowed to thee, O Mighty God of Jacob—and the commandments which thou hast given unto him, and that he hath sincerely striven to do thy will."* Emma knew his words to be true. He *had* seen many afflictions and persecutions, and he truly had striven with sincerity to do God's will in spite of those things. But Emma wasn't prepared for his declaration of this truth *not* to be for the purpose of soliciting God's blessings upon himself, but upon *her* and those most dear to her.

"Have mercy, O Lord," Joseph continued, *"upon his wife and children, that they may be exalted in thy presence, and preserved by thy fostering hand. Have mercy upon all their immediate connections, that their prejudices may be broken up and swept away as with a flood; that they may be converted and redeemed with Israel, and know that thou art God."*

Emma was overcome with unexpected emotion. She felt taken aback and somewhat confused. *Immediate connections?* Was that in reference to her own family members, those loved ones she missed so desperately because she had been expelled from their lives? Oh, how she prayed that they would embrace the truth and know the same peace and joy that she held in her heart!

Emma focused on the remainder of Joseph's magnificent prayer and the unearthly events that followed. But laying in bed that night, she thought again of having herself mentioned in that prayer—and her immediate connections. She pondered the meaning of the words that had been uttered, and asked that the Spirit might help her understand. She prayed for family members who had chosen not to be a part of her life. But deep inside herself she had the sense that Joseph's prayer for their immediate connections had a meaning that included more, and she asked the Lord that she might perceive the answer. Did it mean their posterity? Their children were only three and five years old. Such a prayer was profound and remarkable. But she had to wonder since it had been revealed to her prophet-husband whether there was some cause to be concerned over prejudice sufficient for the need to have it be broken up and swept away. And why, for all they knew to be true, and for all that they would surely teach their children, would there be any issue regarding their conversion and redemption? If she knew her husband to truly be a prophet—and she did—then she had to believe there *was* cause for concern. But in that moment it was impossible to know the reasons.

Emma prayed that for whatever reason Joseph had felt inspired to utter such words, those who were—and would be—most precious to her *would* be converted and redeemed—whether now or in generations to come. Were they not, she couldn't imagine greater heartache. For all that she and Joseph had suffered in this world, the promise of eternal blessings gave her peace. To think of her loved ones not having the privilege of those blessings was heartbreaking. Of course, there was nothing to be done about it now but to keep doing all that she did each day, to raise her children the way God would have her raise them, and to sustain her husband in the great work he had been commissioned to do. She knew that her own place in that work was of great value, as well—not as an extension of Joseph, but as an individual, a

CHAPTER NINE

War

On a Sunday evening, a week after the temple dedication, a crystal-clear series of visions was given to Joseph in the temple. Emma knew the moment she saw him afterward that something wondrous had happened. She could see it in his eyes, in his countenance.

"Oh, Emma," he said in hushed reverence at their first opportunity to be alone, "it's happened. All of the sacrifice . . . the struggles . . . it's all been worth it." Tears rose in his eyes.

"What's happened?" she asked, taking his face into her hands.

"The Lord has accepted His temple, Emma," he said in a voice she could barely hear.

"You *saw* Him?" Emma whispered, incredulous.

Joseph nodded but was unable to speak for a full minute while he struggled for composure. Emma felt his absolute joy seep into her spirit as an undeniable witness of the truth filled her being. He sat down as if he were too weak to stand, and Emma sat beside him, waiting to hear what else he might tell her. "The prophecies have been fulfilled, Emma," he said, and went on to tell her that following the appearance of the Savior, Moses came as well, then Elias, and finally, Elijah—all in fulfillment of things foretold. Oliver had been with Joseph throughout the course of the experience, but Emma felt no less sure of its reality than Oliver surely felt.

Later, Joseph took Emma to the temple and showed her where the visions had occurred. He explained to her more of the meaning of these great events. And while she found joy in all that he said, her mind savored most his telling her of the promises associated with Elijah's appearance. "The time has fully come, Emma, for the hearts of the fathers to turn to the children, and the children to the fathers. Do you realize what this means?"

"Not entirely, no," she admitted.

"Through this work," he said, taking both her hands into his, "all of God's children will have the opportunity to return to live with our Father in Heaven . . . no matter when they might have lived and died. We can do for those who have passed on what they cannot do for themselves, and in turn their hearts are turned to us." He went on to explain the doctrines in more detail. Emma marveled anew at all that Joseph had been taught by heavenly messengers, and at her own privilege of being so close to his firsthand accounts. For many days she pondered all he'd shared with her, marveling again and again. She couldn't help thinking of her family as she considered the implications of all that Joseph had told her. A door had been opened, and God had provided a way for the honest in heart in all the earth's ages to return to His presence. She prayed that would somehow, in some way, include her own loved ones. She prayed harder than ever that her father's heart would be softened, even while she knew that answers to prayers didn't always come in the way or time frame she might desire. Still, Emma often paused to thank the Lord for allowing her to be in this place at this time, and to be given such privileges. It seemed all too wondrous to comprehend, but not at all difficult to believe. Such truths, once burned into Emma's heart, were irrefutable and undeniable, even if she could not fully understand their eternal implications.

With the temple finished, opposition seemed to greatly multiply against the Saints. The temple most certainly offered the Saints the opportunity for many great blessings, but its presence also heightened Satan's efforts to revile against those blessings and the great potential of those who were faithful. Threats and anger became more prevalent—not only from outside the Church, but from within it. Men that Joseph had loved and trusted, men who had stood by his side through glorious events, were becoming angry and bitter as a result of the trials they had suffered, and subsequently were falling away and turning against Joseph *and* the Church. Emma doubted that little could be so painful to Joseph as this.

Emma knelt next to her husband beside the bed while he prayed aloud. She could never count the times they had prayed together, nor could she summarize the concerns and burdens they had shared with the Lord in these moments when the three of them met together. But that night Joseph's prayer expressed the depth of heartache he felt over his brethren in the gospel who were becoming lost in apostasy. Some were angry over misunderstandings and disappointments; others were calling Joseph a fallen prophet and fueling the fires of persecution that were always smoldering. Emma's heart ached for her husband even more than for herself. She too had trusted and looked up to these men. It was an unthinkable turn of events!

When Joseph's prayer was finished, he sat on the edge of the bed and invited Emma to sit beside him. He held her hand close in his, briefly pressing it to his lips, as if he might gain some needed strength by doing so.

"How can this be, Emma?" He leaned his forearms on his thighs while keeping her hand in his. He spoke of the friends and fellow brethren in the Church who had turned against him. He spoke of William, Oliver, and others. He let out a soft moan, and Emma shared his anguish, especially considering the incomparable events that Oliver had witnessed. "Now Parley is wavering," Joseph added. "Who will be next?"

Emma prayed silently for the right words to say, wondering how *any* words could possibly console him. But she did her best to reassure him, reminding him that above all else he needed to remain faithful, no matter what others might do, or how his own heart might be broken.

Joseph looked into her eyes, and together they shared a hundred thoughts in silence. He sighed and looked down again. "The Lord will try His people, Emma; of that I have no doubt. I only pray that they will have the strength to continue trusting in Him—no matter what happens. And I pray . . ." His voice cracked with sorrow. "I pray that . . . those who have turned away . . . will one day return. Oh, what joy I would feel to see them return, Emma."

He put his head on her shoulder, and she put her arm around him, praying that they might one day know that joy.

In the time that followed, Emma prayed very hard on behalf of these friends of Joseph who had turned away. And when she felt compelled to do so by the promptings of the Spirit, she did her best to appropriately reach out to these people and share with them her own convictions, with the hope that it might aid in softening their hearts. She knew from experience that no amount of prayer could alter the free agency of another human being. But she had to do all that she could. Her conscience demanded it.

Emma believed her prayers were being heard when she felt prompted to speak with Parley. She prayed for courage in facing such sensitive feelings, and for guidance to say the words that might touch Parley's heart and help him once again find the knowledge there that had initially brought him into the fold.

Emma's sense of fulfillment was immeasurable when Parley *did* come back, and healing took place between him and Joseph. There was great joy as he and others returned to the fold, and greater anguish and sorrow while still others only grew in their hatred and anger. The spirit of darkness overpowered many. What frightened Emma most of all were the threats against Joseph's life—and those of his family. She believed in her heart of hearts that if persecution would only cease, they could live as well as any other family in the land. But persecution did *not* cease, and Emma wondered if she would merely have to accept that it was their lot in life to bear.

The threats became so great that once when Joseph was warned about his life being in peril, he left without being able to inform Emma. A wedding had been planned at their home, and Emma had no choice but to go ahead and be hostess to the event, trying to remain cheerful and not dampen the mood of the celebration in spite of her concerns for her husband. In time, he was able to return, but the strain began to wear on him, and he became very ill. For weeks he was bedridden, and Emma feared he would not recover. She knew the Saints were praying for him, and many were available to help her care for him, but if he didn't recover, no one would miss him as much as she would. She tried to convince herself that losing him to illness would be better than losing him to some dreaded, violent act. But she didn't want to lose him for any reason—under any circumstances.

Emma heard rumors that Joseph's enemies believed his illness was a punishment from God due to his wickedness as a fallen prophet. Emma knew it wasn't true, but she still cried over the matter, praying that these loathsome men would be proven wrong. When it became evident that Joseph would recover, she counted her blessings and thanked the Lord over and over for sparing her husband. And she prayed that he would continue forward in strength and safety. His enemies were surely disappointed by his recovery, but there were many more who rejoiced. Emma needed him! *The Saints* needed him!

In spite of its enemies' opinions and evil efforts, the Church continued to grow. Membership had expanded from 680 at the end of 1830—the year the Church had been organized—to

13,000 by the end of 1836. An additional great blessing of that year for Emma and Joseph was the arrival in June of another healthy baby boy. Frederick Granger Williams Smith, they called him—named after their dear friend, the doctor of the same name, who also served in the First Presidency with Joseph. Each child that joined their family helped assuage Emma's grief over the children she'd lost and deepened the love in their home.

As time passed, persecution and growth continued hand-in-hand, usually at proportionate rates. Joseph once again had to go to Missouri to handle matters there, and Emma wished the Saints were not in two separate locations, requiring all of this back-and-forth travel by her husband. Hyrum had gone to Missouri earlier, and Emma stayed near his wife, Jerusha, who was very nearly ready to give birth. Mary Fielding, a dear friend, was also there to help care for Jerusha and her four small children.

Following the birth of her fifth baby, Jerusha became very ill. Emma was grateful for Mary's help in caring for Hyrum's wife, along with their children. But Emma's worst fears were realized when her precious sister-in-law passed away, just eleven days after the baby was born. Mary was gracious enough to take on the care of the children; otherwise, Emma didn't know what they would have done. But the loss of Jerusha was traumatic for her. Jerusha was a sister to Emma in so many ways. They were not only married to brothers, but their husbands were united in every aspect of the cause, and were closer than most brothers would ever be. Emma and Jerusha had been equally united in cause, worrying together for their husbands and working by their sides in doing all that was required of them. But Emma didn't have the time or the luxury to fully grieve for the loss of Jerusha. Financial crisis was beating down her door, and in Joseph's absence she was continually being threatened by creditors that her husband's property would be confiscated unless she paid debts for which there was no money to pay. At the very hour when she felt sure all would be lost, the Lord sent someone offering to help. Emma cried without shame in the presence of this good man and graciously accepted his assistance on behalf of her husband.

Joseph's return in December was sweet for Emma. No matter the burdens they shared, it was sharing them that gave her strength. Just to have him with her, and to feel like a family while he treasured time with their children was one of her greatest joys. As always, however, all things were bittersweet. His grief over losing Jerusha was as she'd expected. Not only did he feel the personal loss of his sister-in-law, but he felt his brother's pain. He told Emma more than once that he prayed it never happened to them, that he could never bear losing *her.*

"Oh, I need you, Emma," he murmured and held her close while they cried together in their mourning.

"I need you too," she reminded him. "You must be careful . . . and stay strong, Joseph. We *all* need you."

Jerusha's death was not their only source of grief. Many men were leaving the Church—along with their wives, many of whom were Emma's friends. Such losses put their financial concerns into perspective. Money issues seemed so irrelevant when weighed against the loss of deep trust and affection, coupled with concern over the eternal welfare connected to such choices. It was truly heartbreaking for both her and Joseph. Emma often felt a quiet nagging that perhaps she could have done more, even though she had no idea what more she could have done. Over time she'd come to recognize that nagging voice as the one that always held her back and weighed her down. She'd come to understand its source, and knew well that Satan's influence could distract and distort the human spirit with his evil whisperings. Emma struggled daily to stay close to the Holy Spirit and remain strong. But some days the battle of her own inadequacies, her grief, and the weight of her burdens made it difficult to maintain perspective. Through prayer and service and study she held on, pressing forward, one hour, one day at a time, always hoping that she would not disappoint God, or her husband, in any way.

Later that month, as the year was drawing to a close, Hyrum married Mary Fielding, and she officially became a stepmother to the children she had been caring for. Hyrum and Mary had the common bond of grieving for Jerusha, and Mary truly loved the children. Emma believed it was a good match, and she prayed they could find happiness together.

But trouble was brewing again. Brigham Young actually had to flee from Ohio because he had defended Joseph among those who were dissenters from the Church. It soon became impossible to ignore the severity of the increasing persecution, and Emma knew before Joseph told her that they would have to leave as well.

"How can we leave the temple?" she asked him while a thousand memories of the related work and sacrifice went through her mind.

Joseph's sigh was deep and tortured. Leaving the house of God behind could be no more difficult for anyone than for him. "We must if we hope to preserve our safety." He put an arm around her shoulders and gave her a reassuring squeeze. "God will see Zion built and thriving, Emma. I have no doubt of it. But it may not be in the way—or in the time—that we expect."

Emma lifted her face to his and offered her best encouraging smile. He smiled back, even though they both knew that leaving Kirtland—and its temple—behind would require letting go of a piece of their hearts.

"There will be more temples," he said with a sparkle of something in his eyes that contradicted his heavy countenance. She knew that look. It was the ongoing presence of things that he knew as a prophet of God that no amount of heartache or suffering could suppress. For Emma, the possibility of building another temple felt overwhelming, especially with the financial burdens and continuing opposition. But Joseph had said *temples.*

Did he mean there would be many? While the idea seemed incomprehensible, she trusted Joseph's visions and imagined that such a day when multiple temples existed on the earth would truly be grand. But, as always, the present crept in and had to be faced.

"Will things get better for us if we go to Missouri?" she asked. He took her into his arms and held her close, but he didn't answer. She wondered if for all of being a prophet, he simply didn't know. Or maybe he *did* know and felt it was better left unsaid.

That night Emma lay staring into the darkness, one hand against Joseph's shoulder while he slept. There were moments, such as this, when sleep, for all its necessity, eluded her, and the busy-ness of life relented only long enough to allow her mind to wander through the events that swirled around her and to accept them fully into her spirit. She could understand why some might think her husband wracked with delusions and suffering from madness. But she also knew that any person willing to consider Joseph's stories with an open mind and a willing spirit could know, as she did, that they were true—magnificently and startlingly true. Even now, her spirit trembled at the thought of all that Joseph had experienced in his young life. He had conversed with angels and had been touched by ancient prophets. He had seen God the Father and Jesus Christ in all their glory—face-to-face. And she knew it was true. She could never fully grasp or comprehend such wonders, but she knew they had happened, nevertheless.

Emma pondered the feelings that had drawn her to Joseph in the first place. He had radiated something indefinably wonderful that had drawn her thoughts away from every other man who had sought her attention. Talking with other women about such feminine matters, she knew it was not uncommon to feel so utterly smitten with a man, and to believe he was the finest man on earth—and the only man worth giving your heart to. But Emma's initial attraction to Joseph had quickly become mingled with the realization that he had been chosen by God as the only man on earth in that present day to be His holy messenger. And Emma wondered . . . had she sensed it from the start? Or had she simply fallen in love with him because he was so easy to love? And she wondered more deeply why she, of all women, had captured Joseph's eye—and his heart. As surely as she knew that her husband had seen and talked with God and angels, she knew that he loved her. She knew it because he made it clear to her every day they were together. In word and deed, he made evident his affections for her. He revered and respected her as his equal and did not esteem himself above her. He treated her as Adam had surely treated Eve, as a helpmeet and companion. Of course, Emma didn't consider herself the kind of woman to stand for being treated as anything less. And Joseph had known that from the start. But what Emma *hadn't* known initially was that she'd fallen in love with a prophet of God. How could she, of all women, be equal to a man who was privy to such wonders? She didn't have to be a personal witness of these things to be able to know of their truthfulness. And she didn't need Joseph's continual reassurance of his love for her to know that it was real. In both cases, she was equally firm on Joseph's unwavering integrity and commitment.

Emma suddenly felt overcome with gratitude—that she, of all women, would be blessed with the honor and privilege of standing at Joseph's side, and for the absolute knowledge in her heart that the things he had told her were true. He'd told her he had seen God and spoken with angels. He'd told her that he loved her. It was all true.

Emma turned over and snuggled close to Joseph's back while he continued to sleep. He shifted slightly but slept on. Tears warmed Emma's eyes and soothed away any anxiety over what the future might bring. She believed that the memories of moments such as this would carry her through.

Joseph was forced to leave Kirtland ahead of his family, knowing that his life was in danger. Emma was left to pack their belongings and, without her husband, bid farewell to their beloved Kirtland. They had seen many struggles there, and they had also witnessed miracles too numerous to count. But Emma looked back only once, bidding Kirtland a fond farewell, holding the good memories close to her heart and choosing to lay aside the bad ones.

Little Frederick was just more than eighteen months old when Emma and her children set out in the care of Joseph's brother, Don Carlos. They were now refugees in the wilderness. For two months of winter cold and storms, they crossed nearly a thousand miles of American prairie while Emma could only keep putting one foot in front of the other and doing everything in her power to keep her children warm and fed. The situation improved considerably when they met up with Joseph along the way. Don Carlos then returned to Kirtland to help others make the journey. Joseph was Emma's best friend and her greatest strength on this earth, and she knew she was the same to him. Everything was better when they were together, even though Emma was enduring the ill effects of another pregnancy. But complaining over their circumstances would be a pathetic waste of time that Emma felt no need to indulge in. She only wanted to put this journey behind her. She hoped, if nothing else, that perhaps the Saints would not be so scattered, and that Joseph would not be torn between two locations. Surely good would come from this harrowing exodus; if she couldn't believe that, how could she ever keep going in the face of such absolute misery?

At the border of Indiana, they met up with Brigham Young. Joseph had run out of money, and Brigham helped make arrangements for them to receive financial aid from a kind benefactor willing to help. They found the Mississippi River frozen, but not solid enough to consider it safe for crossing. Brigham and Joseph worked together to find a way to get the wagons and teams to the other side without disaster.

Arriving in Far West brought a relief to Emma that compensated for the less-than-favorable conditions there. Just to not be traveling, exposed to the cold, was a blessing that aroused her deepest gratitude. And most blessed of all was being there with Joseph.

As always, strength was found in numbers. Hope increased for those who had already suffered much in Missouri, as well as those who had traveled far to escape the persecution in Ohio. Life was good in Far West, even though Emma couldn't rid herself of nagging concerns. There had been too many problems in Missouri previously for her to feel entirely comfortable. But she did her best to enjoy the peace while it lasted, praying every day that her family and the Saints would be protected.

Early in June, Emma gave birth to yet another healthy boy. They called him Alexander Hale, and his siblings took great joy in his arrival. Julia was now seven, and a great help to her mother. Little Joseph would be six come November, and Frederick was turning two only a few weeks after the birth of his baby brother. Emma found joy in her children that was only enhanced by the joy that Joseph felt in being their father. *If only life could always be this way,* she would often think during peaceful and tender moments. But in her heart she knew it would not last. She couldn't be sure if such feelings were born of hard experience, or if they were the subtle whisperings of the Spirit, preparing her for more hardship to come. Perhaps they were both. Either way, she had to accept the inevitable. Peace was only a brief respite and had to be enjoyed for the moment while it lasted.

Their reprieve in Missouri proved indeed to be brief. Hatred swelled and overtook the Saints in ways Emma never would have imagined possible. Even as prepared as she had tried to be, she never could have fathomed the reality of such persecution. Then word came that shooting had broken out at Crooked River. Friends had been killed at the hands of their enemies. When Emma realized what had happened . . . when she saw Brother Patten—a dear friend—lying there with a bullet in him, a cold panic grabbed her heart unlike anything she'd ever known. In her mind she could see Joseph there in his place. And the inconsolable grief of his widow was difficult to contend with when Emma could so easily put herself in this woman's position. Was it some kind of premonition, or was it merely fear playing with her mind? Either way, the danger was impossible to ignore. Lives had been lost. When would it end? How bad would it get?

Emma forced her own selfish thoughts to the back of her mind in order to appropriately deal with the situation at hand. She did her best to offer aid and support throughout the crisis of Brother Patten suffering from his wounds, then eventually dying. She managed to keep herself together enough to give the best comfort she could offer to Sister Patten. But the moment she was alone at home, fear and sorrow rushed out of her in torrents. She had hoped to vent the majority of her emotion before facing Joseph, but he found her crying and wrapped her in his arms. He said nothing, but the strength of his comfort filled her. *Oh, please don't take him from me,* Emma prayed in silence while she clung to him, allowing her tears to dampen the shirt that covered his chest. *Just let him live, Lord, and I will do anything!*

After Emma had calmed down somewhat, Joseph took hold of her shoulders and forced her to face him. "Talk to me," he urged gently.

"What is happening, Joseph?" she asked. "I don't understand." With her words she once again became so upset that she could hardly breathe. "Our friends . . . our fellow Saints . . . being shot down and killed in cold blood?' She sobbed. "Is this what it comes to? Are we truly at war?"

Joseph responded to her question as if he'd been struck. He moved unsteadily to a chair and pressed a hand over the center of his chest, as if he were suffering physical pain.

"What's wrong?" she asked and sat beside him, her concern for *him* overriding everything else.

"I fear it *has* come to that, Emma." He planted his elbows on his thighs and pressed his head into his hands. She knew him well enough to know that he'd likely been trying to spare her from worry. But apparently her question had rendered him helpless in withholding his anxiety.

"What's happened, Joseph?" she demanded, her fears heightening. She wanted to be a strength and comfort to him, but she hardly knew what to say when she had no idea what was really going on.

He sighed from within the deepest part of himself and tugged at his hair as if that might help him think more clearly. "There are some among us . . . who have taken it upon themselves—without my knowledge—to secretly mete out vengeance upon the people of Missouri."

"No." Emma barely breathed the word while the possible ramifications of such action plummeted through her mind. She recounted how hard Joseph had worked to promote peace among the people. He'd admonished them repeatedly to defend themselves if needed, but never to be vengeful or be the cause of any unnecessary harm to others.

Joseph wiped a hand over his face. "Many of them were convinced that they were acting under my orders. I fear the responsibility will be laid at my feet . . . no matter the outcome . . . no matter how I've tried to . . ." His voice trailed off beneath a stifled sob. A few moments later he went on. "Even as much as I am against what these men have done, Emma, their crimes have been grossly distorted and exaggerated. The governor is eager to hear false reports, and he will never believe that I was not behind any wrongs committed against his people." He sighed again. "He is an evil man, Emma, intent on destroying the Mormons." He looked up at her, perfect anguish in his eyes. "I fear that you're right. The war between good and evil is at our doorstep."

Emma swallowed carefully and fought for a steady voice. "And will that war be fought to the death?"

"You will be preserved, Emma," he said with gentle confidence, setting a hand to her face.

"How can you know that?" she blurted, and his silence answered her own question. She recalled phrases from her patriarchal blessing so clearly that the Spirit might have been whispering them to her as an echo of the promise she'd just heard from her prophet-husband. *Thou shalt see many days, yea, the Lord will spare thee till thou art satisfied* . . . But she had to ask, "And you?"

"For now. My time has not yet come." He took her face into his hands. His voice as well as his eyes gave her hope. "We must trust in the Lord. For all that He may try us, we are ever in His hands. Those who have lost their lives for His name's sake are the most blessed among us, Emma."

"It's those of us left behind who must suffer most . . . living in constant fear."

"We must *not* live in fear, Emma." He sighed. "I know it's not easy, when there *is* so much to be afraid of. God knows that I *do* struggle with fear." He drew her head to his shoulder and held it tightly there. His voice became ragged. "I ache with worry for you . . . the children . . . all of the Saints. But we must *all* trust in the Lord, Emma. We *must!*"

Emma knew he was right. She also knew that the greatest test of faith came in the most difficult of circumstances. And she had a feeling that for their family—and the Saints—the full depth of that test was yet to come.

The nightmare intensified when word came only two days later that the incident at Crooked River had been grossly misrepresented to the governor, and he had taken steps that were appalling beyond comprehension. It was difficult to accept that, in the United States of America, the extermination of a religious body had been made legal. Emma was so utterly in shock over the news that she had difficulty believing it could be real.

"Surely not!" she insisted to her husband.

"I'm afraid it's true," he told her in a calm voice that she knew belied his internal struggle. He was a prophet of God, and the people who looked to him for guidance were in peril of losing their lives by violent means—that had been made legal. Emma did not envy his position. But she understood the heaviness of his heart.

Joseph feared that with the Extermination Order made public, every fanatic Missourian who didn't like the Mormons would be only too happy to take advantage of the governor's edict and be rid of them. Just three days after the order was issued, Emma was faced with evidence that no longer made it possible to doubt the truth of such a possibility. A massacre had occurred at Haun's Mill, a Mormon settlement just a few miles east of Far West. Nearly twenty Saints had been killed—including old men and young boys. Several more had been wounded, including one woman. Emma knew her own shock and horror could not compare to the growing burden of grief her husband felt. She struggled to console him, but there was far too much drama going on around them to have the luxury of long talks or the time to mourn.

Lying in the dark with Joseph beside her, Emma was as unable to sleep as she knew he was. She didn't like the uncertainty in the air, especially coupled with the dark cloud that seemed to be hovering over them. He pressed a kiss to her brow, and she took hold of him with an instinctive desperation, praying the sensation was not some kind of foreboding.

The course of events unfolding around them did nothing to assuage Emma's concerns, but rather heightened them. She could easily imagine some of the scenes she had read about in the Book of Mormon as Far West was fortified against an inevitable attack from the Missouri Militia. They truly *were* at war, and she wondered if the madness would ever end. When Joseph was informed that the generals wanted to speak to him, Emma was horrified to learn that he intended to meet with them. She felt sure it would be the end of him. He believed that if he could plead his cause to them—if he could convince them that the intentions of the Saints were not violent, but peaceful—that it would improve their standing. Emma wasn't sure that such men could be persuaded to any good. Her nerves tightened further when she knew that Joseph was getting ready to leave. She found him shaving and made no effort to hold back how she felt. "Something's wrong. Joseph, I'm begging. Please don't go."

Joseph rinsed the blade in the basin of water, then hesitated, turning to meet Emma's gaze. And she knew she wouldn't like what he had to say. "If there is any way of stopping this madness . . . how can I not?"

Emma turned her back, if only to hide the way she squeezed her eyes closed and grimaced with her heightening fear. She knew well enough that her desire to keep him home and safe would never make him stay. She knew he was doing the best he knew how under deplorable circumstances. He didn't need her worries and fears to add to his burdens. If she couldn't keep him here, then she needed to send him off well aware of the love she felt for him. She fought to get control of her emotions enough to do so, wondering what she might say. If he left, would she ever see him again? The thought evoked more emotion, rather than subduing it. She swallowed hard, then felt his hands on her shoulders. She knew from the feel of his face next to hers that he'd finished shaving.

"We must keep our faith in the Lord, Emma," he whispered.

"I know," she muttered, her voice entirely lacking the conviction she had hoped for.

"Be strong for me, my darling." He wrapped his arms around her from behind. "Your strength inspires me, you know."

"I'm *not* strong," she said, admitting her deepest feeling and endeavoring to hold back her tears.

"You're stronger than you realize . . . and we will get through this . . . whatever happens."

Emma nodded and turned around to embrace him. They held tightly to each other for a long minute of silence while she willed herself to put forth the strength he needed. She succeeded in holding back her tears until after he left.

Not long after he had gone, Emma's tears were waylaid momentarily by distant noises that threatened to stop her heart. Gunfire and triumphant whooping sent Emma to her knees, groaning and unable to breathe. When the children became upset by her behavior, she attempted some bravery and composure for their sake. But it was short-lived. Word quickly spread through Far West that Joseph and the men with him had been surrounded and taken. All of the Saints—Emma included—felt certain they had been killed. It took every bit of strength Emma could muster to simply care for her children and futilely attempt to console their grief. Frederick and the baby were too young to understand, but they surely sensed their mother's grief. Julia and little Joseph, however, were every bit as upset as she was. Emma could only do her best to comfort and console them, while she herself felt beyond consolation.

Once the children were asleep, Emma had no incentive to show any courage. Throughout the night her anguish overtook her. She had always feared that this day would come, but she was entirely unprepared for the reality. *Joseph.* She said his name over and over into the darkness, wondering how it had come to this, and praying for the strength to go on. By morning she knew that grief was a luxury she could hardly afford. With Joseph dead and the city under mob rule, how would she protect her children? If not for them, she would have preferred death herself; she only wanted to be with Joseph. But the children needed her, and she needed to be strong for them. Still, the anguish was all-consuming, and she found that attempting bravery for the sake of the children was fruitless. Together they cried and prayed, then cried some more. She told them that surely all would be well, that God would be with them, while in her heart she fought to convince herself that it was so. He had taken Joseph's life when Joseph had been so certain that his time was not yet done. She prayed for peace and understanding, but they felt elusive and out of reach.

Emma was confronted with a hurricane of fresh emotion when she heard a commotion outside. She opened the door to investigate, with Julia and little Joseph clinging to her skirts. She was barely able to remain standing when she saw Joseph alive, but her relief was immediately dampened by the evidence of his bondage. She cried out her husband's name and followed little Joseph to greet him, but their son was brutally pushed away by one of the armed guards, and Emma was warned to stay back. Through the few parting words they were allowed to exchange from a distance, Emma had to accept that her relief at seeing him alive was likely just a tiny reprieve. Her grief of the past several hours was surely to be relived at some future point. They were taking him away, and she wondered if she would ever see him again. Seeing him now in the custody of such loathsome men felt somehow worse than believing he'd been dead. Now she had to wonder what unspeakable suffering he might have to endure. Memories of his being tarred and feathered haunted her. A different sort of grief engulfed her, and again she could only try to keep the children calm and struggle to pray her fears away.

With the absence of Joseph and many other men who had either been arrested or were fleeing from that possibility, the situation in Far West only worsened. The people were required to turn over all of their firearms, which left the men nothing to hunt with. Crops had gone unharvested, and these combined circumstances left them with very little to eat. The town was left in the care of hateful men—mobocrats at best—who ransacked homes and helped themselves to whatever they pleased, including the women. Emma felt as if she'd been transported to some other place and time where women and children had to live in constant fear, and where men were dragged from their homes and families for no just cause.

Emma grabbed hold of a tiny spark of hope when she received a letter from Joseph. At least he had been alive to write it, even though she could only wonder what might have since happened to him. Still, she savored every word he'd written, and read it over and over. He expressed trust in her ability to conduct all matters as circumstances and necessities required, and asked that God would give her the wisdom and prudence and sobriety she needed. She was most touched to read, *O Emma, for God's sake do not forsake me nor the truth, but remember me. If I do not meet you again in this life, may God grant that we may meet in heaven. I cannot express my feelings; my heart is full. Farewell, oh my kind affectionate Emma. I am yours forever. Your husband and true friend.*

Just more than a week later, another letter arrived, this one even more filled with thoughts that seemed to have come directly uncensored from Joseph's heart. He wrote of his desire to be with the children, and expressed hope that he might see them before too long. She found hope herself as she could almost hear his voice speaking the words he'd penned to her: *Oh, my affectionate Emma, I want you to remember that I am a true and faithful friend to you, and the children forever. My heart is entwined around yours forever and ever; oh, may God bless you all.*

A few weeks later, on the first of December, the militia leader, Captain Bogart, delivered a note to Emma from her husband. She politely thanked him and tried not to bristle before she closed the door and scrambled to read what was written there. Its brevity was frustrating, but at least she had one more piece of evidence that Joseph was alive. He'd been transferred to a jail in Liberty, but he did say that he and the other men imprisoned with him were in good spirits. She hoped that was true and not simply an attempt to console her and the children. Of course, she'd seen firsthand that Joseph did well at remaining in good spirits in the most deplorable of circumstances. He'd had a great deal of practice with that.

CHAPTER TEN

Driven

The hardships and depravities at Far West continued, while Emma could only do her best to be of any help she could to those who were suffering. But her heart was constantly with Joseph. Concerned beyond description for his welfare, and desperately longing for his company, she was grateful for the opportunity to travel to Liberty and see him.

The journey was long and miserable, made worse by the cold and unpredictable weather of winter. She was not surprised at the repulsive men keeping guard over her husband and the other men imprisoned with him. She'd become quite accustomed to the presence of such men as they continually lingered around the people of Far West, their eyes filled with evil. Emma was, however, shocked by the conditions in which she found Joseph.

Upon her arrival, the basket of food she'd brought was riffled through by a surly guard, reminding her of the many times her home had been invaded and her possessions and property ravaged. A door in the floor was opened to the dungeon below, and a ladder let down. When Joseph painstakingly climbed the ladder, Emma had to suppress the urge to cry out. She'd never seen him look so dreadful. He was dirty and unkempt, and a thick beard covered the lower half of his face. The straw in his hair and on his clothes made the sleeping arrangements evident.

But his relief at seeing her lit his eyes, making the journey more than worth her efforts. Oblivious to anything but the evidence that he was still living, Emma wrapped her arms around him. She held him tightly, luxuriating in the joyful moment of simply being with him, knowing that he felt the same.

"You're so cold!" she observed, speaking softly with the hope that they might not be overheard by the guards lurking nearby.

"I'm all right," he insisted, and they sat close together on a little bench. "How are *you?* I've worried so for you."

"I'm fine," she told him, not wanting to burden him with details of a deplorable situation that he was already keenly aware of—and helpless to do anything about. Emma touched his face. "I need you to stay alive, Joseph. Come home to us."

He put his hand over hers. "I pray every hour that I *will* come home to you . . . my precious Emma."

Emma distracted him with anything pleasant she could think to talk of. She told him things about the children that made him smile, avoiding as much as possible the mention of any details that would only trouble him further. Their visit was far too brief, and they both had difficulty saying good-bye. For all that they steered away from facing it, they both knew there was a possibility they might not see each other again. If not for the children, Emma would have preferred remaining with Joseph—even laying down her life alongside his. But her children needed her, and she needed to be strong for them.

Returning to her home in Far West, Emma was horrified all over again at how lamentable the situation really was. The constancy of fear began to wear on her. She fell asleep each night wondering if she would wake to find her children or herself being dragged from their beds and thrown into the streets, as had happened to Hyrum's wife, Mary. Each day she prayed for strength and blessings enough to see them through, then she did everything in her power to simply keep her children fed and safe and to aid others in their misery as much as her time and resources allowed. And every waking moment her heart ached with worry for Joseph and those who were with him. It was nearly impossible to keep her thoughts away from wondering what they were being subjected to. She knew for a fact that her husband was cold and miserable, and that he was being given food that could hardly be qualified as edible. Atop all the physical depravity he was being subjected to, she couldn't even imagine the depth of his worry and concern for the Saints and for his family. She was worried about that, too.

Emma visited Joseph at Liberty Jail on two other occasions. Each time, she had trouble accepting the fact that weeks had passed and he was still there. And each time she was struck by the deepening misery of the situation of the Saints—both those inside and outside of prison. As always, Emma felt torn between telling Joseph the truth, and sparing him the frightful reality of the condition of the Saints for which she knew he felt responsible.

On her third visit, Emma wondered more than she had previously whether they would ever see each other again. When he inquired over her well-being and that of the children, she had no choice but to tell him. "If I'm going to keep the children safe . . ." she whispered, hearing a tremor in her voice that didn't begin to express her fear, "I should take them away from here." Sorrow broke into her words. "But how can I leave you here like this?"

"You mustn't concern yourself over me. I will be better if I know that you and the children are safe."

Emma knew that he meant it, but upon examining his countenance she was struck with a sobering reality. She'd never seen him so utterly disheartened. She had seen him suffer through much, but he had always found strength from within himself—a strength that had kept *her* going. His despair coupled with her own was surely too much to bear.

Joseph breathed out a weary sigh and took hold of her hands. "Oh, Emma." His eyes expressed perfect sorrow. "You deserve so much better than this." He sighed again. "Perhaps your father was right." He hung his head, and his voice cracked with a depth of sorrow Emma had never heard from him. "He said no good would ever come of it. If you had not married me, then—"

"Don't you say it!" she insisted. He lifted his eyes. "Don't you even think it." Tears overtook Emma. "Much good *has* come of it, Joseph." She took his face into her hands. "I love you, Joseph. I would not choose any other man . . . or any other path." A tentative smile touched his lips as tears slid down his face. Emma wiped them with her thumbs and added, "More importantly, you must remember that I did not marry you, nor have I stayed with you, only because I love you." She looked down and swallowed carefully, unable to deny the truth. "I wonder sometimes if love would be enough; perhaps not." She lifted her eyes again and looked at him squarely, needing to know that he understood the convictions of her heart. "God brought us together, Joseph. It is my mission to stand by you in yours. I know it, and I know that God knows it. And I cannot deny it."

Joseph's eyes softened, and he made a noise that was almost a laugh. She'd heard him use those words many times in regard to his First Vision. When she put it to him that way, there was no need for any further explanation. He knew exactly how she felt. He nodded and touched her face, murmuring amidst the onset of more tears, "Oh, my precious Emma. My heart is entwined around yours . . . forever." He kissed her brow. "Don't ever forget, Emma. Promise me."

"I promise," she murmured.

Emma held that promise and the tenderness of her husband's affection close to her heart as she packed up almost all that she possessed and took her children out of the state. Emma was grateful for the help of friends in transporting their few belongings and giving her family aid in their need to travel. Her greatest concern was for the manuscripts containing Joseph's ongoing translation of parts of the Bible. A sweet friend made a special apron for Emma, with pockets large enough to hold a sizable portion of the pages. She wore it tied beneath her skirts, wanting them to be protected from the weather. The size and weight of what she carried was significant, but she found some comfort in knowing with every step that Joseph's work was safe. She left with the Saints on the seventh of February, praying as always that her children and all those traveling with them would be kept safe and well, and that Joseph and those who shared his bondage would have that same blessing.

No one but God could know the feelings of her heart in facing yet another exodus. Once again they were crossing the frozen Mississippi River, this time heading toward Illinois. Emma wondered why they'd even come to Missouri at all. To her it felt like nothing other than a despicable and evil place, and she could find no comprehension of God's promise that Zion would one day be established there. It would surely take many generations for the hatred against Mormons to be purged from the Missouri soil. Emma knew in her heart, however, that most residents of the state would have likely been appalled if they'd been made aware of the persecution. Those who had behaved so evilly were a minority, but the extent of that evil was widespread and deeply rooted.

For all the misery of the journey, Emma was glad to leave Missouri behind. She found hope in simply leaving its borders. But her resolve to only look forward was difficult when her heart remained behind with her husband. She wondered if it might be possible for the Saints to settle *anywhere* and not eventually be subjected to persecution beyond toleration. But for now, she set her mind on the path ahead, choosing *not* to look back, even while her heart remained in a cold, dark dungeon in Liberty. The word *liberty* would never again mean freedom to her.

After nine days of traveling through icy weather, sleet, and snow, they finally arrived in the Illinois town of Quincy. Many of the Saints became ill due to the hardships of the journey and exposure to the elements, but the people of Quincy were kind and generous in a way that made the mobs of Missouri seem all the more deplorable. As Emma and her children, along with the other Saints, were taken in and given shelter and other necessities, her faith in God was restored, and she knew His hand was present in the lives of His children.

Once the Saints were free from the horrors of Far West and living in a community that treated them fairly and respectfully, the onset of spring brought with it new hope. Emma's relief was deep on behalf of her little family and the many Saints who had suffered so much. But her heart feared for Joseph, and every moment was filled with yearning for his presence and with prayers on his behalf.

Letters were sent to Joseph and Hyrum and the others to let them know of their move to Quincy, and that all was well there. The children were responding positively to the spring weather and the peace in the air, and Emma was deeply grateful. If only Joseph could be with her, she felt sure that she would never complain of misery again. She prayed each hour that it might be so.

It was a thrill to all of the family when a letter arrived from Joseph. He wrote to her, *Affectionate wife, I have sent an epistle to the Church directed to you because I wanted you to have the first reading of it, and then I want Father and Mother to have a copy of it . . . My dear Emma, I very well know your toils and sympathize with you. If God will spare my life once more to have the privilege of taking care of you, I will ease your care and endeavor to comfort your heart.*

His words soothed Emma's spirit and warmed her deeply. She read through all that he had written for the Church, vacillating from explicit sorrow on her husband's behalf to perfect joy at the wondrous revelations that had been received. It was clearly evident to Emma that the despair Joseph had experienced as a result of such unspeakable circumstances had eventually brought him to a corresponding peace as the heavens were opened.

Emma kept the words Joseph had written close to her heart as she helped care for the sick among their people, waiting for the right time to share them with his family. Joseph's father was among those with poor health, and Emma talked quietly with him while she pressed a damp cloth to his fevered face. Not certain if he was facing death, he asked her to look after Lucy when he was gone. Emma promised that she would, but insisted there was no need to worry about such things yet—while in her heart she prayed they would not lose him. He was such a strength to the family, especially in Joseph's absence.

Later, Emma was able to share with the family the things that Joseph had written to her. *"'O God, where art thou? And where is the pavilion that covereth thy hiding place? How long shall thy hand be stayed, and thine eye, yea thy pure eye, behold from the eternal heavens the wrongs of thy people and of thy servants, and thine ear be penetrated with their cries? Yea, O Lord, how long shall they suffer these wrongs and unlawful oppressions, before thine heart shall be softened toward them, and thy bowels be moved with compassion toward them?'"*

Emma paused to compose herself, then read on, intermittently exchanging a comment with family members while they shared a perfect bond of concern for Joseph.

As the sorrow of Joseph's prayer turned to revelation, Emma heard the tone of her voice change and immediately sensed a tangible hope surrounding the family. Her own hope deepened as well, and her heart was comforted at the words the Lord spoke to Joseph.

"'My son, peace be unto thy soul; thine adversity and thine afflictions shall be but a small moment; And then, if thou endure it well, God shall exalt thee on high; thou shalt triumph over all thy foes. Thy friends do stand by thee, and they shall hail thee again with warm hearts and friendly hands.'"

Apparently it wasn't yet time for Joseph's father to leave this world, and Emma was deeply relieved, as were the rest of his loved ones. Emma still missed Joseph and worried for him, but the revelations he'd been given—that she had read repeatedly—had given her perspective and strength.

A few weeks into April, Emma was drawn to look out the door. She had to close her eyes and open them again to be certain they weren't deceiving her. For a moment she feared that the man approaching the house might not be her Joseph. But it was *him!* He looked more ragged and dirty than she'd ever seen *anyone* look. And the hardship and hunger showed on his face. But he was *alive!* He was *here!* A joy that eradicated every bit of fear and sorrow she'd ever known surged through her as she ran out to meet him. She threw her arms around him and held him—possibly tighter than she ever had.

"Oh, Emma," he murmured close to her ear, returning her embrace with meager strength. "Praise be to God for bringing me back to you."

"Amen," she muttered in return and took his bearded face into her hands. "Oh, you're all right?"

Joseph nodded, and they were overtaken by the children. He laughed with perfect delight but didn't have the strength to pick them up as she knew he would have liked. Emma helped him into the house and hurried to prepare a bath. Once he was clean and shaved, Emma smiled at him, saying, "There's the husband I remember." She didn't comment on how thin and sallow he looked. Now that he was back in her care, all would be made right with time. And she chose not to think of all that had happened to put him in such a condition. She knew that forgiveness was vital. Otherwise, they would never be able to press forward.

With a good meal in his stomach, Joseph was able to enjoy reunions with many loved ones, and he couldn't stop talking about how the children had grown and changed. Emma delighted in seeing how glad the children were to see him, even though little Alexander was too young to even remember him, or to understand the hardships they had endured these many months. As Emma considered once again all of the ugliness that had occurred in Missouri, it seemed to her that the Mississippi River had become a barrier between their safety and security and the nightmares left behind there. In her heart she swore that, whatever the future might bring, she would never cross that river again.

Emma had barely become accustomed to having Joseph with her again when she received earth-shattering news in a letter. She went to her knees, consumed with heaving sobs, her hands pressed over her heart, where the pain felt too intense to bear.

Her sobbing brought Joseph into the room, and he immediately knelt beside her. "What is it, Emma? What's happened?"

"My father is dead," she managed to say.

"Oh, Emma," he whispered, "I'm . . . so sorry."

He held her close and whispered assuring words, reminding her of principles of the restored gospel that gave her hope that all was not lost in regard to her father.

Emma found comfort enough in his words to take a deep breath and consider the hope of such a possibility. She knew better than to think that he would say such a thing in regard to her father simply to pacify her. If Joseph said it, she knew it was true.

Joseph was deeply compassionate toward Emma's grief, but as always, there was too much of life going on around them to allow any kind of loss to slow them down. In spite of his poor physical condition, Joseph was quickly engaged in seeing to the needs of the people. He was able to acquire some property not far from Quincy in a town called Commerce, directly on the

Illinois side of the Mississippi River. Joseph reported that it was somewhat swampy, and for this reason it had been all but abandoned. He felt sure that it was a good place for the Saints to gather and live in peace. If they had to take land that no one else wanted, that was fine with him. He felt confident that they could be industrious enough to overcome its challenges and create a lovely and thriving community. Once the legalities had been taken care of, the exiled Mormons streamed into the area, glad to have their prophet free and ready to lead them once again.

Joseph and Emma moved with their children into a small old two-story house made of squared-off logs. Even though it was small and in poor repair, they were together and free from threat and oppression. And Emma couldn't have been happier.

The people quickly proved how hardworking, inventive, and inexhaustible they could be. While living in tents, in wagons, or under the open sky, they set to work clearing farms and building temporary dwellings that would prove adequate until time and resources allowed something better. Joseph worked at least as hard as anyone, quickly regaining his strength and vitality. And he continually reassured the people that their efforts would be worthwhile. He intended to rename the place *Nauvoo,* which in Hebrew meant "beautiful place." For Emma, its greatest beauty was the absence of fear she'd felt in Missouri and the presence of her husband in her life. She prayed that both would last.

They had barely begun to settle in when a terrible sickness moved among the people. The swampy ground along the Mississippi was an ideal breeding ground for a number of illnesses, and their treacherous hand brought many down with a wretched fever. Hardly a family went unaffected. Everyone was miserable, whether ill themselves or struggling to care for those who were. Some died. Emma spent every possible moment caring for the ill, with Julia and little Joseph helping as well. Her husband's weakened state from his recent imprisonment and the ongoing stresses of his life left him vulnerable, and he too became ill. Emma had no choice but to leave her husband in the care of others while she moved among those who needed her attention, returning to Joseph's side as frequently as possible.

Emma straightened her back and wiped sweat from her brow with a dirty sleeve. She turned to scan the masses of the sick and dying and those feebly attempting to care for them. She wondered how she could ever do enough. There were so many—so many who had trusted in the Lord, had trusted in Joseph. They'd come here in faith, and now their misery was only enhanced once again. How could she *ever* do enough? *One moment at a time,* a voice inside her seemed to say. *Just keep doing the best that you can, one moment at a time.*

Emma reminded herself to trust in that voice, even though it began to rain. She entered their little block home to get out of the weather, but found it wasn't much better inside. The roof leaked so terribly that water was dripping in several different places. The house was full to overflowing with the ill who had nowhere else to go. Emma moved to her husband's side and heard him muttering her name as he came out of a fevered sleep. She held his hand while he spoke of the beautiful place this would someday be, with hope that seemed completely unwarranted considering the present situation.

Emma stayed with him until he settled back into a fitful sleep. She looked around at her pathetic surroundings and tried to imagine Joseph's vision. She knew from vast experience how much worse things could be, and she'd become very practiced at counting her blessings. High on the list was having Joseph in her care, and being free from the oppression of the Missouri Extermination Order. Silently thanking God for all they *did* have, she pressed a kiss to Joseph's brow and went back to work, wishing her mind didn't stray so frequently to the loss of her father and the pain it evoked.

Illness raged on, and misery continued. Nevertheless, in weighing all options, Emma would still choose this over the nightmares of Far West and over having her husband imprisoned. While she felt concerned for his health, he was confident that he would recover because his work was not yet finished. Emma shared his confidence. After all, he was a prophet.

A day came when Joseph got himself off of his makeshift bed, in spite of feeling poorly, and went from camp to camp, putting his hands upon the heads of those who were ill and pronouncing them healed in the name of Jesus Christ. Emma followed and watched, too overcome to speak as she witnessed miracle after miracle. Those who had been too ill for many days to even stand up rose immediately to their feet to embrace this great man who held a singular authority from God to work mighty wonders. At the end of the day, he settled his head back where it had rested throughout the course of his own illness, as if his work in the previous hours had been nothing different than that of a farmer or blacksmith. Once the children were settled for the night, Emma laid close beside him, whispering in his ear her love for him.

Joseph turned to look at her and smiled faintly. "You're a good woman, Emma," he said. "And I love you too."

Emma kissed his brow, and they both slept.

With time, Joseph's condition improved, as did that of many of the Saints. However, one of the characteristics of the ague that beset them was its frequent recurrence. Emma herself became afflicted with the illness, and was overcome with the kind of misery that made death seem preferable. And for reasons they didn't understand, the illness would come back out of nowhere and often put the victim down all over again. The fact that many others struggled with the same symptoms gave the people empathy for each other, but it didn't make the matter any easier. Like the others, Emma could only do the best that she could and try not to think about all of the things she should have been doing while she was too ill to do much of anything.

Eventually, the illness became less severe. The people worked hard to drain the swamp, build homes and businesses, and plant crops. Joseph fixed the leaky roof of the house, and they worked together to make it a home. Once again Emma felt grateful for safe shelter and for having her husband close by and doing well.

Just as the sticky heat of summer began to relent, Emma realized she was pregnant. A combination of emotions overwhelmed her. Nothing could make her more happy than to have another child. And she knew that Joseph shared her sentiment. Their children were a living manifestation of the love they shared, and their greatest eternal blessing. But Emma couldn't ignore the possibility that this child, like many of her others, might not live, and they would only be faced with more heartache. She would prefer not being pregnant at all as opposed to going through that again. But she prayed for her fears to relent and focused instead on the hope of having another child join their family.

During the winter months, Emma often compared the present with the previous winter. The contrast left her continually grateful to God for removing them from the torment of Missouri. All around her she saw the Saints struggling to come to terms with the scars left from the mobs' cruelty. But for the most part, the people were faithful and strong, grateful to be alive, and grateful to have their prophet and leader among them. Even though he came and went in order to see to God's errands, he made his presence known among the Saints when he was there, and Emma knew they drew comfort from him, just as she did. Still, no one knew him—or relied on him—the way that she did.

The city of Nauvoo rose quickly under Joseph's direction. He had a clear vision of the work he was to do—nothing less than the building up of the kingdom of God on the earth. And he shared that vision with all who would listen. Converts continued to pour in from other parts of the country—and the world—and the city was thriving. Emma found joy in being part of such a great community, as hearts were knit together in a common cause. Those who had endured hardship and survived it were all the stronger for it, and the bond among them was rooted deeply in the gospel that filled their hearts and governed their lives.

Early in the summer, more than a year after their arrival in Nauvoo, Emma gave birth to another healthy boy. She praised God for His rich blessings, and once again found perfect joy in observing Joseph and the other children with the new baby. The love among them made up for so much. Extended family as well thoroughly enjoyed little Don Carlos—named after Joseph's brother, who was also very dear to them.

As always, Emma often thought of her own family and missed them—both those who were living and those who were dead. Knowing there was nothing to be done about it, she was all the more grateful for Joseph's family, and for the love and acceptance she had found among them. Her husband's parents loved her as their own, and their love of the gospel united them in a glorious cause—a cause that her own family could never understand, only because they had chosen not to even consider the possibility that this man she had married was truly what he claimed to be, and that the gospel he had been commissioned to bring forth was indeed true.

Joseph surprised Emma one day with a wonderful gift—a string of gold beads, perhaps the most lovely necklace she had ever seen.

Emma touched the beads as she admired them, sharing a smile with her husband. From that day forward, she wore the beads nearly every waking hour. They were priceless to her as a visible reminder of Joseph's love.

That September brought the death of Joseph's father. In spite of all they had come to learn of the gospel plan, and the hope they had of being reunited in the life to come, watching him pass away tore at Emma's heart. The grief at his death was sharply contrasted, however, by his final words, as he whispered that he could see Alvin. All who were with him knew that it was true, and it added validation to the vision that Joseph had seen years earlier. There was joy in thinking of father and son reunited on the other side of the veil, but the separation for those left behind was difficult. Emma shared her husband's sorrow over the passing of this great man who had been to her the father she'd always wanted her own father to be. Father Smith was greatly honored among the family and the Saints for the distinguished man that he was and the marvelous contribution he had made to the work of the gospel going forth. His support of Joseph had always been unequivocal, and his service to others unmatchable. He would truly be missed. Offering comfort to Lucy over the loss of her husband, Emma hoped that she might be at least as old as her mother-in-law before she ever had to face losing her own husband.

Losing Joseph's father couldn't help but open Emma's wound of losing her own, and she was surprised at how much the loss still tugged at her. She was grateful to be able to share her deepest feelings with her husband, and each day she prayed and struggled to find peace over her father's death. Joseph was continually empathetic to her sorrow. He now understood the loss of a father, but he had the peace of knowing that his father had loved and supported him, and that they'd been unified in the gospel cause. When time permitted, Joseph told Emma again of the marvelous revelations he'd received that had taught him much about life after death and the plan of salvation. He assured her that her father would continue to progress and yet have a chance to hear the gospel message. Emma knew what he said was true; she could feel it in her heart. Yet it didn't take away the sorrow of separation, nor the disappointment of having her father die without ever giving her the approval and acceptance she had yearned for. But it did give her hope. And she had learned the value of hope through many experiences in her life. Without hope of eternal blessings, she couldn't imagine having any hope at all.

The city of Nauvoo grew as quickly as did little Don Carlos. Their own little house was fixed up and then added onto, and Emma was content there—at least as content as any woman could be with a continual stream of company coming and going from her home. Her kitchen was used as the Church office, and there was almost always something going on there. Homes and shops were rising in abundance, and crops were flourishing. The river boats were frequently stopping at Nauvoo, often bringing new converts who were anxious to meet the famed prophet and settle in his city. Emma was not unaware of the deference that followed her wherever she went. Being publicly known as the wife of Joseph Smith was not without its challenges—and its pleasures. She had learned from vast experience that she was in a position to do much good, and to personally testify of the truths that she knew her husband stood for. She only wished that her every action might not be under public scrutiny. She would have far preferred a much simpler, more quiet life. But this was the life she had chosen, and she would do her best to make the most of it. Or perhaps it was more accurate to say that God had chosen *her* to live this life, and she would do well to honor Him in every possible way.

Daily life was certainly not without its challenges, but comparatively speaking, Emma felt continual gratitude that it was good. And she refused to entertain any thought as to whether or not their peace in Nauvoo might eventually give way to the same fear and persecution they had endured in the past. She wanted once again to believe that she and Joseph could grow old here together with their children around them, and with a temple in view. Nothing could make her happier!

CHAPTER ELEVEN

Beautiful Place

Emma was just beginning to think that she could eventually find peace over her father's death when tragedy occurred once again. Joseph's brother Don Carlos died from illness, leaving behind a wife and children. Emma felt as devastated as her husband. She had known Don Carlos since he was nine, and he had done much to help care for her and the children during difficult times when Joseph had been away. But they barely had time to address their grief before little Don Carlos—ironically named after his uncle, now barely in the grave—became suddenly ill.

Fear gripped Emma's heart when she realized how sick her baby really was. She paced the floor with a frantic helplessness while his screaming deafened her, and the fevered temperature of his skin was impossible to ignore. The more he cried, the more her inability to console and comfort him tore at her mother's heart. At fourteen months of age, he was heavy to hold, but she felt oblivious to the strain in contrast to her fears.

As the gravity of Don Carlos's state became more severe, the battle inside Emma raged. Memories of her babies' deaths haunted and frightened her—most especially the death of little Joseph. Unlike the others, he had lived. He'd been healthy and strong. And then illness had snatched him from her. Against her will, she found her mind recounting the events leading up to his death, how she'd felt the life slipping from him. Recalling the horror that had happened to Joseph in the midst of it made her struggle for breath while she paced. He'd been in so much pain, was so wounded and battered, while little Joseph had been steadily growing weaker. Emma reminded herself that Joseph was strong, and she refused to consider the ever-present possibility that someone else might do such unspeakable harm to him. Instead she focused on Don Carlos, refusing more firmly to even consider that God might take him from her as well. "He won't!" she muttered to herself amidst her feeble attempts to soothe the baby's wails. "He wouldn't do this to me." She thought of the joy little Don Carlos had brought to all the family, to all who loved him. He was barely fourteen months old. Surely it couldn't be so serious! Surely he would be all right!

Realizing what a state she'd worked herself into, Emma reasoned that a frenzied mother could never calm an ailing baby. She prayed and dug deep for any strength she could muster inside herself that might motivate her to faith. She talked herself out of the fear, over and over, until it overtook her once again. Still the baby cried, and still she paced the floor. Joseph finally returned home and immediately took the baby from her. But he only cried harder, and his father's attempts to help were pointless when Emma could not separate herself from her baby's suffering. There was nowhere to go where she wouldn't hear his cries, if only in her head.

"Let me do it," she insisted, taking him back. She hadn't meant to sound abrupt with her husband, and hurried to add, "I'm grateful for your help. I just . . . need to do it."

He nodded and eased Don Carlos into her arms. His helplessness was evident, but for that very reason, Emma felt prey to an anger she didn't want to admit. She knew she was frightened and too tired to be sensible. But she also knew her husband was a prophet of God. She *knew* it. He'd healed other people's children. She'd seen it with her own eyes. Why not theirs? Why not now?

Continuing to walk the floor, she told herself it wasn't fair or right to put such a condition on him. But at the moment, her fears were stronger than reason. Joseph remained close by, visibly distressed, helpless, and clearly as worried as she. He walked the room as well, at a less frantic pace but equally aware of their baby's anguish. He gave the child a blessing, but there was no mention that he might be healed—or live. And again the routine began. Emma's internal battle resumed, and she wondered if she were simply responding to a deep paranoia born of the previous losses in her life. Or if the Spirit might be preparing her to face the inevitable. The very idea urged her emotions to the surface, and she heard herself telling Joseph that God would not take another one of her babies. He would *not!* He said nothing, but she saw his chin quiver and tears form in his eyes. She wondered if he knew what the outcome would be. She wondered if she knew it herself but was too angry and afraid to accept it. Again she told him, as if doing so might make it real, "Promise me that he will not die!" She ranted and paced, patting Don Carlos's little back. "Promise me!" Hearing her own words and their tone, she wondered what kind of madwoman had overtaken her. Her deepest fears rushed out of her in heaving sobs, contradicting her determination to keep this child alive. Joseph wrapped his arms around both of them, but his attempts to soothe her could not change the reality. A few hours later, Don Carlos was gone.

"Why, Joseph?" Emma asked. The absence of the baby's crying felt stark and eerie. "Why can you save other children, and not your own?"

She knew the question pricked him by the way he squeezed his eyes closed, grimacing as if he'd been struck. She turned to look the other way when his obvious distress only threatened to lessen the shock that was protecting her own anguish. But she needed an answer. She wasn't blaming him for this. She just needed an answer. And while a part of her already *knew* the answer, perhaps she just needed to hear him say it.

"It is not my will, Emma, but God's . . . that heals the sick." She heard him choking on his tears, barely able to speak. "It is not within *my* power to govern God's purposes—or to question them."

Emma wasn't surprised by his answer, but she still felt angry. In her deepest self, she knew her anger was only a mask for the unfathomable hurt of so much accumulated loss. But in moments of such raw grief, she found it impossible to be brave or strong. She didn't want to have to say the right thing or search for strength. She could only feel the pain, and in that moment, she couldn't imagine ever being free of it.

Suddenly finding it difficult to breathe, she rushed outside, as if the fresh air could fill her lungs with something that might vanquish this unbearable reality. She didn't know how long she stood by the river, unable to cry, unable to accept that yet another baby was gone. Only when Joseph appeared by her side did she realize how much more she needed to be with him than she needed to be alone. Even in the painful silence, she felt the tiniest measure of solace in knowing that her deep grief was shared.

"Talk to me," he muttered, his voice hoarse with evidence that he'd been crying long and hard.

Vacillating between extremes of irrational emotion, Emma wondered what she could possibly say that wouldn't hurt him. She had grieved before, and she knew well enough that the anger would demand most to be heard initially. But she felt *more* angry this time, more wounded, more confused. She knew there was no one to be angry with. Joseph had been right in what he'd said. It wasn't his fault. And she couldn't be angry with God. She could, however, admit that she was having trouble understanding His need to take her children from her. She knew, because Joseph had taught her, that the gospel he was fighting so hard to restore to the earth gave them the knowledge that they would have their babies again, that these losses would be made up through the Atonement of their Savior. She knew that what Joseph had said was true. But eternity was so difficult to comprehend while her mortal arms ached with emptiness and her mother's heart felt cracked and utterly broken.

Emma's roiling thoughts finally brought her to the question she needed answered. She swallowed carefully and drew her shawl more tightly around her shoulders, determined to keep her tone even enough to disguise any angry feelings that might be hurtful to her husband. Then she chose to simply remain silent. There was nothing either of them could say to change the circumstances. They both had a choice. They could become angry and bitter, or they could choose to go forward with faith.

Joseph too said nothing. Surely, the loss was equally deep for him. Yet, for all Emma had lost, she still had Joseph by her side. He'd suffered much, and they had endured many painful separations. But he had been spared, and she was grateful. Even now, with nothing to say between them, she knew he shared her grief; no one knew better the reality of these losses than he did. And she loved him for it. She felt the tiniest glimmer of hope that she could survive this loss, as she had the others—only because Joseph was by her side. *Please, Lord,* she prayed, *whatever happens, don't take my husband from me.*

"Emma," Joseph whispered behind her ear, taking her shoulders into his hands, "I love you; you are the choice of my heart."

He turned her to face him, and she cried against his shoulder while his own tears dampened her hair. He was her best and truest friend.

While struggling to cope once again with her empty arms, Emma prayed that God would one day replace and mend the broken pieces of her heart. Joseph had taught her that all things lost would be restored, and that it was possible for loved ones to share eternity. Since Emma had by now received word of her mother's death as well, the hope of the gospel became all she had to hold on to.

Emma hummed a hymn as she went about her daily duties. She pondered Joseph's teachings, asking the Lord to help her remember that this was one of those times when, in her mind, she had to separate her husband from the prophet. If she were any other woman who had come here, believing in the Book of Mormon and the restoration of the gospel, Joseph would have given her the very same assurances in regard to the loss of loved ones. Emma knew that for Joseph, her losses were more personal to him—but that didn't change the truth of the principles. She knew in her heart that he was not simply patronizing her, or searching for words that might give her some abstract kind of hope. He was a prophet of God, and she knew that what he'd said was true. Her losses *would* be made up. She wanted to believe that, and prayed that she would not doubt it.

As was her custom, Emma turned her thoughts to the future. The fact that she was pregnant again did not necessarily ease her grief, however. Until she had a living, breathing baby in her arms, she wasn't certain she could anticipate the arrival of this one without risking her fragile heart once again. But then, Don Carlos had been born healthy and had thrived for many months. She knew that death could reach out and snatch away loved ones as quickly as evil could squelch peace and security. She could only live one hour, one day at a time, keeping a prayer in her heart that whatever God required of her, she would be able to face it with faith and an ever-burning knowledge that her life was in His hands.

Emma didn't let her own grief hold her back from doing her part to build the kingdom. There were always needs to be met on behalf of her family as well as the Saints, and a temple was once again being built. There was work to be done, and no time for a woman to sit around and feel sorry for herself. She, of all women, had many blessings to count, not the least of which was being privy to the ongoing events that encircled her husband continually, making it impossible for her to forget that he was being guided by God's divine hand.

As Nauvoo flourished, socializing became more a part of their lives than it ever had been. Emma was reminded of pleasant times in Kirtland as dances and many social gatherings were held. But Nauvoo was already so much larger, so bustling with life and activity. She enjoyed many different interactions with friends and fellow citizens of their beautiful city. But she especially appreciated social affairs where she had the opportunity to dance with her husband. Being waltzed by Joseph Smith was a privilege she adored. And he often made her laugh. Sharing laughter with Joseph never lost its savor.

In February Emma gave birth to a boy who never took a breath. Once again she and Joseph buried a child, and once again she had no choice but to set her grief aside and move on. She had living children who needed her, and a husband whose work consumed him continually. Emma followed his example of remaining busy. Sometimes at night, when rare moments of quiet were available to them, they would talk about their lost babies and cry together. Emma treasured such moments. In the busyness of life, and the need to share her husband with the Saints who were constantly looking to him for leadership, such tiny reprieves were among her greatest blessings.

Not many weeks after putting their sixth baby in the ground, Emma was distracted from her grief when she became caught up in a wondrous and inspired endeavor. Some ladies in the area who were regularly involved in assisting those in need came up with the idea that they should be officially organized in doing so. A proposal was written up and given to Joseph, who reviewed it and complimented them on their desires. But he told them that the Lord had something more in mind, and he asked that they meet together and discuss the matter. At this meeting, Joseph declared that the Church could not be completely organized until the *women* were thus organized. The brethren left the room after giving the women an assignment to vote in order to choose a president for their new society. Emma was surprised and deeply touched when she was voted into that position. Yet in her heart she felt a rightness about it; she knew it had been a part of God's plan for her all along.

The brethren came back into the room, and Emma could see that Joseph was pleased that she'd been chosen—but he didn't seem at all surprised, which deepened her conviction that the call had come from the Lord, even if it had come through indirect means. It was difficult for Emma to remain composed as Joseph read aloud the revelation that had been given to her years earlier. She could see now that the Lord had known of her abilities and mission long before she had, but she also had the distinct impression that these words that had been given specifically to her also applied to all women, everywhere. She felt certain the Spirit was guiding her to such thoughts when Joseph in essence said the very same thing.

After much prayer and pondering, Emma chose counselors and a secretary to aid and guide her, and the Nauvoo Female Relief Society became official. Their regular meetings commenced, and Emma enjoyed deep fulfillment as well-planned and organized charitable projects commenced. Wanting to be an example of all she expected the women of Nauvoo to be, Emma consciously considered the qualities they should strive for, and taught them boldly, always praying in her heart that she could be all that the Lord would have her be. The theme that she felt inspired to follow as a guideline was "Unity, Purity, and Charity." She taught the women to forgive and be charitable, not to gossip but to do good, and to follow the pattern of the priesthood as they supported the brethren in their work.

The Relief Society organization contributed greatly to Emma's personal fulfillment and happiness, as it did to the well-being of the community. Nauvoo continued to grow and thrive, and happiness was abundant.

Joseph's mother was actively involved in the Relief Society, and Emma loved working side-by-side with this great woman in many endeavors. Lucy's example of charity was surely beyond compare, and Emma was deeply touched to hear her say to the sisters, "We must cherish one another, watch over one another . . . and gain instruction, that we may all sit down together in heaven."

Emma was well aware that everyone who knew Lucy looked up to her, but few women knew her as Emma did. She had become the mother that Emma had lost, and she felt certain the closeness they shared was rare.

While Emma was nursing Lucy through an illness, she was given time to ponder all they had been through together as well as their common bond of affection for Joseph. She was reminded of the story of Ruth and Naomi in the Bible, and the commitment between the mother and wife of a good man. But Emma prayed that they might never be in the same position as those women—needing to strengthen each other through the death of that man. She thought instead of the privilege she felt in her connection to Lucy.

Lucy was soon back on her feet, but before long Emma was again afflicted with a relapse of the ague, and her mother-in-law was caring for *her.* They talked often about what they would ever do without each other. Emma didn't even want to think about it.

Emma enjoyed some of the happiest times of her life in Nauvoo. Joseph too was happy and content, and he did well at spreading hope wherever he went. He taught that happiness was the "design and object of our existence" . . . and that it would be the end thereof if people would only pursue the course that led to it. He exemplified his teachings every hour, and people were naturally drawn to him, eager to get near the contagion of his laughter and affinity for fun. Children loved to see him coming, and it took little to get him involved in their play. As always, adults eagerly engaged him in conversation, as entertained by his wit as they were enthralled by his gospel teachings.

There were drawbacks to his popularity, but Emma learned to smile and appreciate each moment, grateful every day that he was alive and not behind prison bars. And after all these years of experience, she finally just made it clear to him that he'd do well not to even try to work in the garden. He was never out there for long before men were gathered around him, wanting to glean his wisdom. These gatherings always resulted in more harm than good—at least as far as the garden went. But it was easy for Emma to understand that Joseph was on the Lord's errand and that his work encompassed something unique and magnificent. A man like Joseph certainly *should* spend his time in such conversations. With each such seemingly insignificant exchange, Emma felt sure that Joseph was building the kingdom just a little more.

Emma could hardly complain about his lack of accomplishments in the garden when he was so good to help her around the house and with the children. Even the teasing of other men could not thwart him in making it known that he respected and honored his wife enough to share her most menial chores. For that, and a thousand other reasons, she loved him beyond all description.

Of course, such tranquility was fleeting, and no one knew that better than Joseph Smith—or perhaps his wife. Word came that the governor of Missouri had very nearly been killed by some unknown culprit, and he was laying the blame at Joseph's feet. Joseph had been nowhere near Missouri at the time, even if he *had* been the kind of man to do such a thing—which he was not. But the governor was so intent on having Joseph extradited to Missouri that he soon had officials in Illinois investigating the matter. Joseph had no choice but to once again go into hiding. Emma was left to face matters that were terrifying. There were bounty hunters searching diligently for Joseph, and her fears were difficult to subdue.

Emma fought away dread and anger, but there were too many nightmarish scenes in her memory to not have them trigger her fear. She hated having Joseph away for any reason, but matters of Church business were simply a necessity. This was entirely different, and she hated it!

She was thrilled with the opportunity to travel with Hyrum and some of the brethren to see Joseph. When they arrived at their destination, Emma followed Hyrum into the woods, her heart pounding at the thought of seeing her beloved Joseph.

"I never imagined we would be meeting like this," Emma said once they'd exchanged greetings.

"It was never in my plans either," Joseph countered with a chuckle.

"I'll give the two of you some time," Hyrum said, and Joseph took Emma's hand, guiding her to walk at his side along the edge of the river.

Emma felt renewed as she was able to spend time with her husband, however brief it was. And she couldn't deny satisfaction in knowing that Joseph felt the same. Giving him strength and hope in the face of his trials seemed one of her greatest gifts.

Emma was able to visit Joseph one other time during his exile, but the danger was too great for her to risk it more than that. Time dragged while their separation became wearisome and difficult, not just for her and the children but for all the Saints. During a particularly difficult time, Emma ached so deeply for her husband's company that she wondered how she could possibly go on without him. The children had been ill, and she'd been struggling with illness herself. It all just felt like too much! Suppressing her sorrow for the sake of the children, she gathered them around her after supper and read to them as their father would have done if he had been there.

Emma considered it a miracle when Joseph was able to sneak home long enough to give the children a blessing. And just being with him, if only for a matter of hours, replenished her spirit and gave her the strength to go on.

When it was time for him to leave, he gave her a letter for the brethren, but told her to read it first. Emma cried after he left, then with the sun streaming through the window, she tilted Joseph's letter toward the light and read, *What do we hear in the gospel which we have received? A voice of gladness . . . a voice of mercy from heaven . . . glad tidings for the living and the dead. Shall we not go on in so great a cause?*

Emma read all that he had written, then held the pages against her heart, counting herself blessed to be the woman he loved and to know that he was safe. She prayed that he would remain so, and that soon these ridiculous charges against him would go away so they could be together, openly and freely.

In time the danger *did* pass, and Joseph was able to once again go about his life and his business without fear of being arrested and taken back to the nightmare of Missouri. Still, Emma could find plenty to worry about without too much effort. But she tried *not* to worry, because there was also much good to think about and with which to keep herself busy. The temple continued to rise, and converts came to Nauvoo at a steady pace as a result of the great, far-reaching missionary efforts in many lands.

With Joseph free and their sixteenth wedding anniversary at hand, it seemed a good time for a celebration. They hosted a grand party at their home, and Emma thoroughly enjoyed being surrounded by friends and loved ones to mark these great milestones in her life. During the celebration and long afterward,

Emma pondered those sixteen years with Joseph and all they had endured and shared. She loved him more than she would have ever thought possible at the time she'd married him. And she knew that he loved her too. She would not trade away her joy with him in order to be free of the hardships.

As winter eased into spring, it became impossible to ignore the persecution sprouting up around them. It had always been present to some degree, and the Saints—for the most part—had learned to live with it. Emma, like many others, had learned to deal with its effects, to help others through it, and to keep pressing forward. She couldn't imagine any situation being as bad was what they'd seen at Far West, and so long as it didn't reach such proportions, she could be grateful and keep perspective. Still, it seemed there was always a cloud on the horizon, and Emma couldn't think about it too long or too hard without becoming frantic over wondering what the future might bring. Unable to live that way, she trained herself to live only in the present. Emma kept doing what she had always done in daily meeting the needs of her family and those around her, determined to be happy and praying that they would all remain safe.

CHAPTER TWELVE

Choosing Faith

Nauvoo had truly become a beautiful city, and the temple rising in the midst of it promised to be a magnificent structure that would stand as a witness of the sacrifice of the Saints and the blessings of eternity God had promised in return. Joseph and Emma were able to move in to the new Mansion House that they'd been building, and the children were well. They passed their seventeenth wedding anniversary, and life was good—as long as they could remain in some tiny little cocoon that might completely shut out the rest of the world. But of course, that was impossible. The storms of adversity threatened to close in from every side, and the warmth of spring only saw matters worsening.

Spring gently met with summer, then the expected sticky heat came upon them. For days Emma sensed an added burden on Joseph. As always, she asked if there was anything she might do to help, or if he needed to talk about it.

"Not now," he said with troubled eyes, "but thank you."

Emma pressed a hand over the side of his face. "You know I would do anything to ease your burdens, Joseph."

He looked as if he might cry as he put his hand over hers and whispered, "I know, Emma—which is one of many reasons you are so dear to me." He kissed her and added, "You are most precious to me, Emma; don't you ever forget."

Emma felt unsettled over the conversation, wondering what might be troubling him that would spur him to clarify his feelings with such emotion. Had he been given some foreshadowing of the future that would add strain to their lives? Would he again go to prison? Or worse, was his life drawing to a close? Emma couldn't even consider the possibility, and she told the Lord over and over that if he would only spare Joseph's life, she could endure almost anything. In her heart, she knew it was true.

A few days later, Joseph told Emma he needed to speak with her. The gravity of his countenance was unnerving, and she wondered if this would be the end of the conversation they'd started earlier. He closed the door and insisted that she sit down, but he remained on his feet, pacing and wringing his hands. She'd never seen him so nervous—or upset. She had witnessed his survival of horrific persecution and betrayal. She had seen him face prison and illness and the hatred of mobs. She'd been by his side through the deaths of many loved ones as well as disappointments unimaginable to most people. He'd struggled with grief and sorrow, with worry and concern, as any man would. But always he'd remained firm and steadfast, taking on all that the Lord required with conviction. Then what could have gotten him so upset? Again her mind went to the possibility that he might have foreseen his own death, or some other evil that might come upon them. And again she thought that if he could only be preserved, if they could only be together, they could surely endure whatever else they might have to face. They had endured and survived enough to certainly prove that.

"This cannot be put off any longer, Emma," he said, still pacing. "I have prayed and prayed that it might not come to this, but the Lord has made it irrefutably clear that I must heed his commands in this, or I will be cut down."

Emma took a sharp breath, not certain if she was more disturbed by the quavering intensity of his voice or the words that he'd spoken.

"Just . . . sit down . . . and tell me," she insisted quietly, her heart pounding.

Joseph did sit down. He looked directly at her and she sensed him drawing courage. Then he looked away and squeezed his eyes closed tightly. She knew he was praying.

"Just . . . tell me," she repeated.

He cleared his throat, opened his eyes, and told her with tears in his eyes what the Lord was asking of them. Emma was so shocked and alarmed she could hardly breathe. She told him what she thought, and he told her where he had to stand if he were to remain in good standing with the Lord. Emma couldn't believe it. After all they had been through, all they had suffered and sacrificed, all they had survived, they would be required to do this. Of all that had been restored by the Lord's hand, Emma never would have imagined that He would deem it necessary to reinstate the biblical doctrine of plural marriage. Joseph and Emma talked on and on, sometimes arguing, sometimes crying.

He vacillated between the firmness of a prophet who knew what God required of him, and a tender husband whose heart was breaking. In the end, it was his tearful plea that remained most prominent in her mind—and in her heart. "Emma, what would you have me do?"

When there was nothing more to say that hadn't already been said at least once, he went out of the house and was gone for hours. Emma cried and prayed and struggled. With time she came to know beyond any doubt that the edict had come from God; if she hadn't known for herself, she never could have lived with it. And she wouldn't have. But she had to live with it. If God required a broken heart to be saved, He certainly had hers.

Emma prayed and studied the scriptures harder than she ever had in her life, begging God to give her peace and strength. She believed she had gained some insight as to how Abraham must have felt when God asked for the sacrifice of his only son. How could you absolutely know in your heart that the command came from God and that it must be obeyed, and at the same time have it threaten to tear your very heart out? A part of her knew that God had great compassion for such pain and sacrifice, and that it would be counted well at judgment day. But contending with such feelings in the present consumed her with grief so raw that it couldn't be examined too closely. Her mind went also to Mary, who had been required to give up her Son. How her woman's heart must have broken to see Him nailed to the cross and suffering, all the while knowing it was what God required! In the grandness of eternity and its promise of sweet blessings, the matter certainly took on a broader perspective. But did Mary give much thought to such things in those moments of immeasurable mortal suffering? The pain had surely been so great that she comprehended nothing but the pain.

Emma was grateful for the strength she was blessed with to bear her burden with quiet dignity. She knew in her heart that only God—and Joseph—truly knew how difficult it was for her. But if that was the price of having all the eternal blessings that Joseph had taught her about, then she was willing to pay it.

Standing alone by the river, Emma considered all that was good in her life; at the same time she wondered what paths they might be required to follow now. Joseph found her there and immediately said, "We need to talk."

Emma turned to look at him and knew by his countenance—and his hesitation—that he needed to say something he didn't want to say.

"Are we leaving again?" she blurted without thinking. "Leaving another city, another temple?"

Joseph sighed and looked toward the river. She felt sure he would confirm her suspicion. Instead he said, "Not you, Emma. You finally have a home of your own . . . a place that is yours. And you must stay."

Emma was relieved on one count, but she'd clearly heard the underlying message. "Where are *you* going this time?" she asked, unable to count the months he'd been away from her, for reasons that were equally difficult to number.

He looked at her then with that prophetic intensity in his eyes that, to this day, left her breathless—but at the same time it frightened her. "The Lord is going to let me rest for a time, Emma."

She gave herself a long moment to process what he'd said, but still had to ask, "What do you mean?"

Joseph sighed again, and this time looked at the ground. "I'm trying to tell you that . . . I don't know when . . . for certain; I don't know how, but . . . I believe my time here on this earth . . . is coming to a close." Emma sucked in her breath and couldn't find the ability to speak before he went on. "I have many enemies, Emma—outside of the fold, and . . . within it."

"But . . . God has protected you, Joseph; He's preserved you . . . over and over. Surely He will continue to do so."

"Emma," he took both her hands into his, "my time is known only to God. And when that time is done . . ."

He didn't finish the sentence, and Emma was left attempting to fill in the missing words. It took a long moment for her to accept them, and even longer for them to be absorbed into her spirit. Now, more than any other moment in the life they'd shared, she wanted him *not* to be a prophet. If he had no divine means of foreseeing events to come, then he could have no intuition that his life was drawing to a close. As the meaning of his words settled into her spirit, she wondered if she could *ever* accept the possibility that he might truly be called on to offer up his life for his beliefs. How could she even consider being able to go on without him?

"So, you are truly willing to lay down your life for this cause?" she asked, sounding more upset than she'd intended.

He answered firmly and without hesitation. "If that's what God requires of me, yes."

His declaration was so difficult to take in that her own jumped back at him on the wave of a sob. "So, you give up your life, and what do I give up?"

They both knew the answer, even though neither of them said it. By giving up Joseph, Emma would give up what mattered most to her. She would be left alone to care for their children and keep them safe. The fact that she was again pregnant only added more irony and concern to the situation. Would he die and leave her to face the birth and raising of this child alone? Or perhaps it wouldn't be so soon. He'd said he didn't know when, that his time was known only to God. Still, it seemed evident that she was being given the opportunity to prepare, even if such a thought was unthinkable. How could she ever be left alone to protect their interests and contend with the growing adversity? Facing *anything* without Joseph felt unthinkable, but he was telling her that the likelihood was inevitable.

She turned her back to him, if only to hide her tears. He wrapped his arms around her from behind, but neither of them said anything more. There was nothing to be said that would make any difference.

Emma had long ago grown accustomed to the fact that in direct proportion to the blossoming of the work and the rolling forth of the kingdom, there was evil underfoot and at every turn. But taking in the deeper meaning of that along with Joseph's declaration, she was continually battling fear and distrust. Opposition was coming from every direction, and

Emma didn't know whom she could trust anymore. The issues had become complicated and overwhelming, with politics laced into religion until Emma herself hardly understood what was happening. Joseph talked of going away, of finding a new place to live. He felt it was perhaps better to separate himself from the Saints; that maybe they would be safer if he were not in their midst. Emma preferred that over having him dead, but it was still a difficult choice to make.

Joseph and Hyrum left Nauvoo, believing it was the right thing to do. But the people were alarmed, and Emma couldn't bear the thought of them saying that Joseph was a coward. So she wrote him a letter, explaining the situation, repeating what she'd heard others say. She asked him to come back. She felt certain he would be all right, that he would be protected as he had been before. But writing that letter became a decision that she struggled to live with for the rest of her life.

1876

Emma's mind wandered back to those final months of Joseph's life. Looking back, she wondered if she'd known all along that it would happen, that she would lose him. But at the time, she'd struggled with even considering such an idea. Instead of concerning herself too much about the future, Emma had learned by hard-won experience to remain in the present, to find joy in a joyful moment, and to find strength to endure a difficult one.

One of Emma's dearest and most precious memories was the day that she and Joseph were sealed for time and all eternity. Joseph's brother Hyrum had performed the ordinance, and it was a truly joyous event for all of them. Emma had felt as much in awe then as she did now that the precious and profound doctrines and ordinances that made it possible for what was bound on earth to be bound in heaven had been restored through her prophet-husband. She found it a source of wonder and joy to consider that the very thing that had given her the knowledge that she and Joseph could be together forever would bless millions of lives throughout the world and the eternities. How could she *not* find joy in that? Emma knew in her heart that for all that God had required of them, she *was* the choice of Joseph's heart. And she knew they *would* be together forever, that they would stand side by side throughout eternity. Knowing *that* kept her pressing forward and gave her peace. Still, there were other memories that haunted her.

"Sometimes I wonder whether he might still be alive if I had done something differently," Emma said.

"Why?" Julia was astonished. "Why would you ever think that, Mother?"

Emma looked toward the window. "I should have never sent him that letter, asking him to come back."

"But what else could you have possibly done? The people were suffering."

"Yes, we were suffering. But we'd suffered before in his absence. Perhaps some believed that if Joseph faced the charges, the mobs would let up. I should have known from experience that could never be true. But I let their fears sway me. I couldn't bear the thought of people calling him a coward; Joseph was *never* a coward. His courage was beyond comprehension." She went deeper into thought, and her voice softened. "Perhaps some believed that if his blood were spilled, we would have peace."

"That could never be true either, could it, Mother." Emma sighed and absently fondled the gold beads around her neck. Julia came beside her and added, "You must forgive yourself. It's not your fault that he was killed, Mother. His life was in God's hands; surely his death was, as well. Perhaps there was no other way."

Emma looked up at her daughter, understandably surprised. A smile spread over her face. "Listen to you . . . telling *me* that God is in charge of our lives."

Julia shrugged, but she also smiled—albeit barely. "Perhaps He is," she admitted and stepped closer to the window.

"I remember the day Father left for Carthage," Julia said, her voice heavy.

Emma remembered it well—perhaps too well. It was one of those days that had felt dreamlike at the time due to the intense emotion she had been suffering. Her memories of it were clear, but they were clouded with a sensation that still made it difficult for Emma to believe it was real. And Joseph's absence in her life since that time had felt equally unreal, as if it were all wrong, and perhaps one day she would wake up to find that they were together again, and it had all been just a temporary separation.

1844

Joseph and Hyrum came back to Nauvoo, even though they both believed that if they answered the call to go to Carthage, they would never leave there alive. Emma convinced herself that God would protect them, that Joseph's time had not yet come. The temple wasn't finished, and the Saints needed him. *She* needed him. Surely he would be given more time!

Emma knew that Joseph and his brother would be leaving for Carthage the following day. She kept her anxiety concealed during the evening, not wanting to upset the children by her own uncertainty—or Joseph's. She suspected their farewells would be difficult, but at least the children would rest well tonight. After the children were down for the night, Emma found Joseph and Hyrum talking quietly. She hadn't intended to overhear, but once she did, she couldn't make her presence known without making it clear that she was crying. As she heard them discussing their feelings about going to Carthage, she had to keep her hand pressed over her mouth, unable to move, barely able to breathe.

Hyrum concluded by saying, "If you go, then I will go with you."

Emma could hear Joseph's voice break as he added, "What a faithful heart you have, Hyrum."

Emma heard a chair slide and took advantage of the noise to slip away. Alone in her bedroom, she vented her tears and tried to tell herself that this would not be the end. She got ready for bed but couldn't sleep. Eventually Joseph found her there, unable to sleep himself. She held to him tightly while neither of them had anything to say.

Emma hardly slept that night. She lay staring into the darkness, frequently pressing a hand over her rounded belly, praying that her baby would live, and that its father would live to hold it in his arms.

The following day, Emma asked Joseph for a blessing, but time was short and he told her to write a blessing for herself, and on his return he would sign it. She prayed that meant he would return.

Farewells were excruciating. Emma lost all hope of keeping the children calm when she was beside herself with grief, not caring who might see her or what they might think. It was as if the entire city of Nauvoo shared her sentiments. Did they all sense it? Were they all afraid that their prophet would not return?

"You're coming back!" Emma said to him, as if she could order him to do so and counter whatever God's will might entail.

Emma wondered after he was gone if her feelings were some kind of indication or warning that she truly would never see him alive again. Had her spirit sensed what her mind had refused to accept? When word came that her husband—and his brother—were dead, Emma felt as if the earth itself had been ripped out from under her. The ironies and paradoxes of their deaths added to the dreamlike—rather nightmarish—sensation of the days and weeks that followed. There was not one of the Saints who didn't grieve deeply for the loss of the prophet and his brother. Lucy lost two of her sons, and every member of their families mourned and reeled in search of some kind of balance when there seemed to be none. Emma knew their feelings, but she felt them far more intricately than anyone could ever fully understand. Losing Joseph was like losing a part of herself, a piece of her heart, a fragment of her soul. She couldn't imagine ever finding her balance again. But she did. She found it the way everyone else found it—through the gospel that Joseph had given his life for, the Saints found a rock to hold on to. And so did Emma.

1876

Emma wiped away her tears and felt Julia's hand on her arm. "You still miss him," Julia said.

"I've never stopped missing him," Emma said, "never stopped loving him."

"I can't imagine how hard it must have been for you . . . how hard it must still be."

"I wonder what I might have done differently," Emma said, as any woman might have. Still, through the ensuing silence, Julia wondered how a woman so strong and noble as her mother could look back and believe that she could have done any better. She'd remained firm and true in the midst of circumstances that would have broken most women. And yet, her woman's heart still doubted her own strength. Julia understood that feeling, and perhaps that was what helped bond her to her mother most of all.

"I wonder that about myself," Julia admitted, "but I've never been as strong as you."

"You're much stronger than you think, Julia."

Julia made a scoffing noise; not out of disrespect to her mother, but at her utter disbelief over such a comment. "I don't feel strong at all."

"Oh, but you are," Emma said with quiet serenity. "It takes a great deal of strength and courage to walk away from a man who is damaging to your well-being. God does not approve of his daughters being treated in such a way. He is surely offended by such behavior, when a man does not honor his stewardship over a wife as he should. And when a woman knows in her heart that she has truly done all in her power to solve the problems, she can also know that He is with her in such difficult choices."

Julia pulled her shoulders back a little, intrigued by the idea.

"Society does not smile upon women who speak too freely or stand away from what's expected," Emma continued. "And society certainly does not make it easy for a woman to divorce her husband in this day and age. But you've done that, because you did all that you possibly could, and you knew in your heart there was no other way. It's a difficult step to take, and I'm proud of you for taking it. Your Father would not want you to be mistreated in such a way; He would not want you to stand for such abuse."

"Do you mean my—"

"I mean your Heavenly Father, but Joseph would agree." A smile touched one corner of Emma's mouth, and her eyes took on that familiar distant quality. Julia was not at all surprised when Emma's fingers reached for the beads encircling her throat to caress them, as she often did when she thought of Joseph. "He strongly approved of a woman speaking her mind."

"It was surely one of the things he loved most about you."

Emma's thoughts returned to the present, and she shifted her eyes to Julia. "Perhaps," she said, a barely discernible break in her voice. "Although . . . I wonder if there were times when my outspoken nature didn't cause him grief."

Julia felt confident in saying, "I don't believe he would have wanted you any other way." A thought suddenly occurred to her, and she felt compelled to say it, "He knew you were not the kind of woman to stand for being treated unfairly."

"Yes, I suppose he knew that."

"*You* are the one who raised me to feel that way about myself, Mother. It was your example that gave me the strength to walk away from the abuse." She paused and felt a little afraid to ask the question that came to mind, but it wouldn't leave her. "Why didn't *you* walk away? Why didn't you leave him?"

Emma was clearly startled by the question, perhaps even offended. Her eyes brimmed with tears, and her voice cracked with emotion, "Your father never treated me unfairly, Julia. Why would you believe that?"

"Others say he did; that his motives were less than admirable."

"Others do not know him the way I did. I would have *never* chosen any other life."

"But it was a hard life, Mother; *deplorable* in many instances."

Emma leaned forward in her chair, and Julia wondered if she'd ever seen her so intense. Her eyes sparked with a conviction that took Julia's breath away, even before Emma said, "I loved him, and he loved me. We love each other still, and we will for all eternity. But love alone could not have seen me through those difficult and deplorable times, Julia. If I'd had the tiniest inkling that Joseph's motives in the choices he made were not based in his obedience to God . . ." she shook her head, "I don't know if I would have remained by his side." The conviction in her eyes deepened, as did the tremor in her voice. "Don't misunderstand me. I believe in the sanctity of marriage, and the need to remain committed through the trials and grief of life's experiences. But it was knowing that God was a part of our marriage that gave me the strength to hold on when it seemed that even the love we shared wasn't enough. Joseph gave everything to serve God, Julia, even his very life. How could I have *ever* chosen any other path than to stand by him? It was *never* easy. But even with my sometimes flailing faith, and all my self-doubt and heartache, my love for Joseph never wavered, nor did my knowledge that God's hand was in our lives. He died a prophet, Julia; I know it! And he lives on. We *will* be together again. I would not have given up eternity with your father for any earthly gratification of my own selfishness. Thankfully, the Savior's grace is sufficient, Julia. Sufficient for me, and for you. He knows the desires of our hearts, and He carries us. I know it, Julia. I know it."

Julia had nothing to say. Her own tears confirmed the truth of all her mother had spoken. Even with her own floundering faith, she felt the tiniest measure of hope on her own behalf for the first time in many years. For all the confusion and heartache of her own life, how could she not be inspired by the example of her mother? She was truly one of the greatest women who had ever lived, and Julia thanked God for the day He had placed her into the arms of Emma Smith.

John Taylor wrote that Joseph Smith had done more, save Jesus only, for the salvation of men in this world than any other man that ever lived in it. And Julia agreed. There were some things she had trouble believing, but not that. She knew it was true. And she had seen firsthand what he had suffered for that cause. Pondering the present, Julia became intrigued with the idea that if her father was so great a man—and he was—what kind of woman would be his equal? God would not have entrusted such a man to just any woman. She would have to be of incomparable character and unfathomable strength. And she certainly was. Their coming together had not in any way been coincidence. God had chosen Emma to be a prophet's wife, and

Emma had stood by Joseph's side through circumstances and tribulation that would have overcome most women, or sent them running. But Emma had remained firm. And for all of the confusion of opinions and hearsay regarding her life, one fact stood out plain and clear and without dispute. She knew her husband had been a prophet of God until the day of his death, and she knew the beliefs he had stood for to be true. She had known it of her own accord, and that knowledge had carried her through. However old age and the weariness of an unusually difficult life may have affected her, those facts were expressly clear to Julia, and she did not doubt them.

Julia stayed on with her mother after that. While Emma was becoming more feeble with age, Julia was struggling to understand her own health problems. But physical maladies aside, being under the same roof with her mother once again helped Julia more fully understand her example and wisdom. She was beginning to find the truth in what her mother had said, that faith was a choice. And her mother had clearly chosen it.

Julia had heard her father say that he'd be willing to walk through hell itself—barefoot if needed—for a woman like that. She believed that there would never be any need to leave the realms of heaven where he surely was now in order to find a woman so angelic in character. For as long as Julia could remember, she'd been well aware that her mother had a gift to love. When little David Hyrum was born a few months after Joseph's death, Emma's love had been unrestrainedly lavished on him. And Julia herself had been a recipient of that love all of her life. Countless others had, as well. Julia, more than most people, had spent her life observing the remarkable charity her mother had always had for others, in spite of her own hardship and suffering. Emma had truly lived her life as a disciple of Christ.

Although human and imperfect, as even His disciples of old had been, Emma had never wavered in her testimony of the Savior, and she expressed that each day in the way that she lived. She had never let her own heartache override her compassion for others.

As Julia sensed her mother's life winding down, she often pondered the course it had taken. They had reminisced extensively about the life Emma had shared with Joseph, but Julia was also keenly aware of the life Emma had lived since her father's death. To this day, Julia only had to think back to that day to feel the reverberations of the shock. It seemed as though the world had stopped, or at least it had for her and her brothers—and especially for their mother. With Joseph and Hyrum both gone, the loss cut deep into the family as a whole. And while they found strength in sharing their grief, they had all suffered so much that it seemed there was little to draw strength from. Julia had been only thirteen at the time, but she had not been unaware of the complicated mass of issues left in the wake of the prophet's death. Emma had known there were traitors among Joseph's friends, but she didn't know who they were. She became assaulted with theories of betrayal and conspiracy to such a degree that she truly had no idea what was real or whom she could trust. Afraid that the same kind of fanatics who had murdered her husband might not be content to stop there, Emma's situation had been grievous, to say the least. As young as Julia had been, she'd observed much and knew more than most how difficult her mother's decisions had been following that grim and terrible day in June of 1844. But not even Julia could fully know her mother's heart. No one could—no one but God, and her precious Joseph.

Still, through all the heartache and grief, Emma's charitable nature never wavered. Julia had observed the daily tender care that her mother had given to Lucy, Joseph's mother, for as long as she was alive. Emma and Lucy were as close as any mother and daughter could be; their bonds were deep and eternal. Julia hoped that she could be the kind of daughter to Emma that Emma had been to Lucy. There was no finer example than that. It was those truly Christlike characteristics of Emma that left her standing tall above other women. In her quiet, simple way, she lived as she knew her Savior wanted her to. Her example of charity and strength spoke as clearly to others as did the profound sermons of her prophet-husband. Even in her frailties and struggles, she had always managed to come through with dignity and grace.

Julia was with her mother through the final moments of her life. Only a few days before her death, Emma reported that she had dreamt of Joseph coming for her. She had put on her shawl and bonnet to go with him, and he had shown her through a great mansion with many rooms. She spoke of him being in the presence of the Savior.

When Emma passed from this life, after living twice as many years without Joseph as she had lived with him, the final words on her lips were clear and undeniable to all who were in the room. *"Joseph . . . Joseph . . . I'm coming."*

Soon after her mother's death, Julia found something her mother had written many years earlier. Once she'd realized what it was, she'd wanted to be alone to read it, to savor every word. Her mother had written down the blessing she wanted after Joseph went to Carthage. But it was never signed. Still, Julia knew in her heart that all her mother had wanted was hers. Imagining her parents together in that very moment, Julia read the words Emma had written on that terrible day in June:

I desire the Spirit of God to know and understand myself . . . to comprehend the designs of God, when revealed through His servants without doubting . . . I hope to perform all the work I covenanted

ABOUT THE AUTHOR

Anita Stansfield with Katharine Nelson on the set of Emma Smith, My Story, *also a project of the Joseph Smith, Jr., and Emma Hale Smith Historical Society.*

In August 1994, when I was asked by the Joseph Smith, Jr., and Emma Hale Smith Historical Society to write Emma's story, I began a course that I never would have imagined. It's been a path strewn with opposition and challenges, but I would not trade away such a privilege for anything in the world. I would be amiss not to offer my humblest gratitude to the many people who aided me along that path. I'm grateful to all of the cast and crew of the film *Emma Smith, My Story,* who allowed me the opportunity to step a little closer to history as I learned about the beloved lives of Joseph and Emma. Especially to Gary Cook, for his unending friendship and support. I'm also grateful to the Historical Society for giving me this rare opportunity, and for the support and guidance along the way. I offer a special thank-you to Gracia Jones, the great-great-granddaughter of Joseph and Emma, and the ultimate expert on their lives. Without your knowledge I never could have done it. And of course, to Mike and Darcy Kennedy, eternal friends and blessed cheerleaders. I also need to thank everyone at Covenant who rolled so gracefully with the punches of getting all the details ironed out, and going boldly with me into this new territory. I thank my family and friends for enduring with me—especially my dear husband. And I offer my deepest gratitude to Joseph and Emma Smith for allowing me the honor of being Emma's voice in this small way. It is my prayer that this book will come forth in the proper spirit to honor them and the lives they lived, and that their sacrifices will be more widely recognized and appreciated. And to every descendent of Joseph and Emma, I wish you great peace and happiness as you come to more fully understand the great legacy from which you come.

Anita Stansfield

The Joseph Smith, Jr., and Emma Hale Smith Historical Society works with the Joseph Smith, Jr., Family Organization to promote understanding of the life and times, teachings, and heritage of Joseph Smith, Jr., and Emma Hale Smith. Its purposes include the sponsorship of educational and religious conferences, accumulation and preservation of historical artifacts, promotion of research and scholarship, publication of historical research and materials, and other undertakings of similar nature. All net proceeds from this book will be donated to this cause.

If you are interested in making a donation, please send it to 595 West 800 South, Alpine, UT 84004.

For more information, go to www.josephsmithjr.org